# Locked and Loaded

McIntyre Search and Rescue

Book 5

by

April Wilson

Copyright © 2024 April E. Barnswell/
Wilson Publishing LLC
All rights reserved.

Proofreading by Sue Vaughn Boudreaux, Michelle Fewer, Lori Holmes, and Adelle Medhi

Cover by Steamy Designs
Photography by Reggie Deanching
Model: Taylor King

Published by
April E. Barnswell
Wilson Publishing LLC
P.O. Box 292913
Dayton, OH 45429
www.aprilwilsonauthor.com

ISBN: 9798305119923

No part of this publication may be reproduced, stored in a retrieval system, copied, shared, or transmitted in any form or by any means without the prior written permission of the author. The only exception is brief quotations to be used in book reviews.

No part of this book may be used in training any artificial intellligence tools or software. This book is 100% human created.

This novel is entirely a work of fiction. All places and locations are used fictitiously. The names of characters and places are figments of the author's imagination, and any resemblance to real people or real places is purely coincidental and unintended.

Books by April Wilson

## McIntyre Security Bodyguard Series
*Vulnerable*
*Fearless*
*Shane–a novella*
*Broken*
*Shattered*
*Imperfect*
*Ruined*
*Hostage*
*Redeemed*
*Marry Me–a novella*
*Snowbound–a novella*
*Regret*
*With This Ring–a novella*
*Collateral Damage*
*Special Delivery*
*Vanished*
*Baby Makes 3*
*Wrecked*

## McIntyre Security Bodyguard Series Box Sets
*Box Set 1*
*Box Set 2*
*Box Set 3*
*Box Set 4*

### McIntyre Security Protectors
*Finding Layla*
*Damaged Goods*
*Freeing Ruby*

### McIntyre Search and Rescue
*Search and Rescue*
*Lost and Found*
*Tattered and Torn*
*Dark and Dangerous*
*Locked and Loaded*

### Tyler Jamison Novels
*Somebody to Love*
*Somebody to Hold*
*Somebody to Cherish*

### Daddy Detectives (Tyler and Ian) Novels
*Daddy Detectives Episode 1*
*Daddy Detectives Episode 2*

### A British Billionaire Romance Series
*Charmed*
*Captivated*

### Miscellaneous Books
*Falling for His Bodyguard*

Audiobooks by April Wilson

For links to my audiobooks, please visit my website:

www.aprilwilsonauthor.com/audiobooks

# 1

## *Robyn*

As I turn the corner onto my street, I notice the lights are on in the apartment I share with my roommate, Ricky. My stomach knots, as this is one more red flag in a recent avalanche of red flags.

It's only ten P.M., and Ricky doesn't get off until eleven. He shouldn't be home. We each work two minimum-wage jobs, and it's barely enough to pay the bills. He knows better than to take off early. We need every penny we can get.

I'm just now getting home from my job as a server at a local diner. I have barely enough time to change clothes and grab a bite to eat before I head to my next job stocking shelves overnight at a small grocery store.

After parking near the back door, I shut off my engine, but instead of getting out, I sit here. I know I'm procrastinating, but I don't want to think about going inside. I don't want to face Ricky.

Things haven't been going well for us lately. He's been acting strangely, distant one minute, manic the next. I have my suspicions as to why, but it's not something I want to admit even to myself.

Ricky and I have a complicated history. We were in foster care together from the age of ten, living in the same house, facing the same challenges. He was like a brother to me. He was my protector. He watched out for me. He confronted the bullies who made fun of me in school. He had my back.

He also slept on the floor beside my bed every single night to keep our foster father—Doug, the pervert—from *bothering* me. He was—*is*—the closest thing I have to family. And now, he's not.

Something's changed.

Something's different.

And I'm afraid I know what it is.

We aged out of the foster care system at the same time, and neither one of us had anywhere to go, so we stuck together. We lived in a family shelter for a while, working whatever jobs we could get until we'd saved up enough money to put down a deposit on an apartment—this apartment.

But lately, Ricky's been *off*. He's been distant and secretive. He's been making hushed phone calls in the middle of the night. He's hardly ever home anymore.

I'm afraid for him. I'm afraid for me.

I've been around enough addicts to recognize the signs. I just don't want to face the truth. He's all I've got, and if he's doing drugs, then I've lost him. He knows how I feel about the stuff. I lost my mother to a drug overdose when I was ten. And my father is rotting in prison for the rest of his life on drug trafficking convictions.

Drugs destroyed my life. They're the reason I ended up in foster care.

And now I'm pretty sure Ricky's going down the same road.

Hoping to avoid him, I come through the back door into the darkened kitchen. I can see a flickering light coming from the living room, which means he must be watching TV. I also hear his muffled voice. He's on the phone.

I sneak down the hallway to my bedroom, slip inside, and carefully close my door. Only then do I risk turning on my light. I strip off my diner uniform and shoes, and then I grab a pair of jeans and a long-sleeved T-shirt from my closet. Just as I'm pulling on my sneakers, there's a knock on my door. My heart rockets into my throat.

"Robyn? You in there?"

*Shit!* "Yeah. I'm changing for work."

My bedroom door opens, and Ricky steps inside, a beer bottle clutched in his hand. He's a mess. His shaggy blond hair is filthy. His clothes are stained. One look at his dilated pupils and glassy eyes confirms what I was afraid of—he's high as a kite. He's doing drugs, probably meth. My heart hurts so badly I could cry.

He smiles. "I'm glad you're home. I been waitin' to talk to you."

"Sorry, but I've got to leave again for work."

He frowns. "No, wait! Forget about work. I got some really big news."

"What are you doing home, Ricky? You should be at work."

He shakes his head. "Nah."

"What do you mean, no? You know we need every penny—"

"That's just it, Robyn." There's a huge grin on his face. "We don't. Not anymore. I got somethin' better lined up for us."

My stomach knots, and I feel sick. "What are you talking about?"

"I got us a deal. A *huge* deal. We do this one thing, and we'll make more in two days than we would normally make in an entire month."

"Ricky, what are you talking about?"

"I met this guy—I've actually been working for him for a few weeks now. And he's got a job for us."

"Us? What do you mean, *us*?"

"Yeah, us. I can't do it myself because my license is suspended. But you can do it."

"Do what, exactly?"

"It's nothing really. No big deal. You just drive up to Seattle, deliver this guy's merchandise to his business partner, and then come right back home. It's a nineteen-hour drive one way. You can make it there and back in two days. Piece of cake."

"*Merchandise?* Don't you mean drugs?" He's talking about delivering drugs. I shake my head. "Ricky, you can't! If you get caught—" His driver's license is already suspended because of multiple traffic violations—speeding tickets, a drunk driving charge, even a minor hit and run.

His eyes are twitching now, which makes him look a bit demented. "I didn't say *I'd* be the one making the delivery. But *you*—law enforcement won't profile you. A pretty young girl? No way. If you get stopped by the cops, just smile and bat your lashes at them."

"*Me?*" I'm horrified that he would even think of asking this of me. My entire body tightens, I'm so angry. "Are you out of your mind? You know how I feel about drugs! There's no way I'd have any part in this. My mother's *dead*, and my father's in prison for the rest of his life—"

"This isn't about *them*. This is about *us*. It's about our future, our financial security. Robyn, we can make a ton of money doing this. The shipment is sixty pounds of meth. Do you know how much that's worth on the street? I'm talking easily millions. Our cut—"

"I don't give a shit about the money."

His expression hardens in an instant, and when his eyes narrow on me, fear trickles down my spine. Ricky's made me uncomfortable before, and he's made me worry, but he's never made me afraid. Not until now.

"You don't get it, Robyn. You have to do this. I already told Verne you would. He doesn't want me doing it. He says I'm too conspicuous. And he can't do it because the DEA is breathing down his neck. But you? He says you're perfect. Cops won't be too suspicious of a pretty girl like you."

"Verne? Who's that? Your dealer?"

Ricky's demeanor changes once more, and now he's all smiles. His eyes light up. "Don't you see, Robyn? This is our big break. No more struggling to pay for groceries. No more worrying about bills. This is our ticket. I'm talking easy money. All you have to do is drive to Seattle. Verne's contacts will handle it from there. And we'll get paid a fortune for just two days of your time. It's a no-brainer."

I can feel my heart breaking. "Ricky, you know how I feel—"

"Grow up, Robyn." The smile is gone, replaced by a coldness I've never seen in him. "I'm not asking you to take it, or even sell it. You're just delivering it. That's all. Your hands are clean."

"Bullshit!" My eyes fill with tears. "No, Ricky. I won't do it." My mind is racing. If this is the track he's going down, it's time for us to part ways. He's the only friend I have in the world, and I'm losing him. Now I'll have no one. I will literally be alone in the world.

Ricky grits his teeth. "I already told Verne you'd do it. You can't say no. He's counting on us."

"*Us*? You mean *me*, right?" I shake my head. "No, Ricky."

"You can't bail on me, Robyn. Verne will—"

"I don't care what Verne will do. I said no."

As I start for the door, Ricky grabs my arm and pulls me around to face him. He backs me into a corner and wraps the fingers of one hand around my throat, tightening his hold, not enough to cut off my air, but enough to get my attention. His eyes harden. "No isn't an option, Robyn."

I don't even recognize the guy standing in front of me.

"Verne's guys are on their way over right now," he says. "As soon as they load the merchandise into your car, you'll drive it up to Seattle, meet with Verne's contact, and then head back home."

*Now?* I shake my head. "How could you do this to me? We used to be a team. What happened?"

His blue eyes narrow on me. "Life happened. Reality happened. I quit my warehouse job two weeks ago. We need this money."

My stomach drops like a stone. "You quit your job? Why didn't you tell me?"

"Because I knew you'd act like this. It's easy money, Robyn. Be reasonable."

"It's illegal!"

Ricky rolls his dilated, twitchy eyes at me. "Stop being such a princess."

The hand around my throat tightens until I can't draw in any air. *I can't breathe.*

His eyes narrow on me once more. "I'm not asking you, Robyn. I'm telling you."

I start to see flashing lights in my peripheral vision, like tiny fireworks. I feel lightheaded, and my lungs feel like they're going to burst.

He reaches back and pulls a gun from the waistband of his jeans and presses the hard muzzle to my cheek. "We don't have a choice, Robyn. I already said we'd do this. And Verne's not the kind of guy who takes no for an answer. This is happening tonight. Nod your head if you understand that."

I nod. I have no other choice. I want to breathe again.

Ricky releases my throat. "Smart girl. I'll call and let them know we're ready. You'll leave as soon as they load the stuff into your car. I'll text you the address in Seattle."

As soon as Ricky walks out of my room, I grab my backpack out of my closet and stuff it full with whatever I can easily grab—another pair of jeans, a couple of T-shirts, a sweatshirt, underwear, socks. I slip into the hallway bathroom and grab my toothbrush, toothpaste, and shampoo. As I'm packing, I can hear him on his phone in the other room, making arrangements.

With my backpack slung over my shoulder, I grab my jean jacket and purse before I slip out the back door. I'm in my car and backing out of the driveway when the door crashes open and Ricky runs outside, wildly waving his arms.

"Robyn!" he screams. "What the fuck!"

I don't dare stop. I pull out onto the street and my tires squeal as I drive away. I have no plan. No idea where I'm going. I just know I need to get out of Denver before I end up a statistic like my parents.

When a chill sweeps through me, I crank up the heat. It's early October, and winter comes early in Colorado. I could kick myself for not grabbing a warmer coat.

All I have is the money in my purse—twenty dollars from today's tips. That's it. I got paid yesterday, but the rent came out automatically this morning, so there won't be much left in my bank account. I stop at an ATM and withdraw the last forty dollars in my account.

Half a tank of gas and sixty bucks. That's all I've got. I have nowhere to go, but I know I can't stay here. I head for the nearest highway on-ramp and head west, needing to put as many miles between me and Ricky as I can.

I jump when my phone rings. As Ricky's name shows up on the screen, I send the call straight to voicemail. He calls again, almost immediately after, and I reject the call.

He sends a text message.

**Ricky: get back here right now! i mean it. get your ass back here**

I ignore him. Another message follows right after the first one.

**Ricky: i'm serious robyn you don't want to cross this guy he's dangerous**

I put my phone on silent and keep driving because what other choice do I have? I keep one eye on the road ahead of me, and one eye on the rearview mirror, as if I can feel the boogeyman breathing down my back. Surely, they won't be able to follow me. They have no idea where I'm going. Even I don't know where I'm going.

Still, I keep an eye on the rearview mirror, watching the road behind me.

# 2

## *Robyn*

It's after midnight, and I'm driving along a deserted highway when my '94 Honda Civic starts to shudder and shake. I smell something burning and I hear grinding noises coming from underneath the hood. This can't be good. My fears are confirmed when the car abruptly loses power and begins to slow. I have just enough time to pull onto the shoulder before the vehicle rolls to a complete stop. The engine's still running, but when I press the gas pedal, it just revs. There's no forward motion.

I smack my palms on the steering wheel. *Shit!*

With a sigh, I put the vehicle in park, turn off the engine, and lean back in my seat.

*I'm screwed.*

I haven't even made it out of Colorado, and I'm stranded.

It's pitch black outside, no moon whatsoever. I look around and see nothing but ominous shadows where huge pine trees line both sides of the road. I'm in the middle of nowhere. I had a vague plan to head west, to get away from Denver, and then turn south and drive to somewhere warmer. Arizona maybe? I'm playing this by ear.

My stomach is in knots. How could Ricky do this to me after everything we've been through? I didn't even recognize the guy I saw tonight. That wasn't my friend talking. That was a stranger. An addict. A desperate one.

When I pick up my phone, I see I have no signal. I'm in the middle of nowhere Colorado, surrounded by trees and mountains. Of course there's no signal. I couldn't call for help even if I could afford to.

My stomach growls, reminding me I didn't have time to grab anything to eat before I took off. And I didn't think to bring a water bottle with me. I have no food, no water. Nothing. And to top it off, I need to pee, badly.

My heart nearly stops when a dark SUV pulls up behind me, headlights flooding the interior of my car, blinding me. There's no way they followed me. It's impossible. I'm on the verge of a full-blown panic attack when the vehicle behind me starts flashing red and blue lights.

*It's just a cop.*

A man wearing a tan uniform and a dark brown cowboy hat exits his vehicle, approaches my window, and knocks.

I roll down my window. "Good evening, officer." I smile up at him and try to act natural.

He shines his flashlight into my vehicle, quickly sweeping the front and back seats. He looks surprisingly young. Maybe he's in his late twenties, not that much older than I am. He's got dark blond hair peeking out from underneath his hat, and a trim beard covers a square jawline. His name tag says *Sheriff C. Nelson*.

"Good evening, miss. What seems to be the trouble here?" His tone is surprisingly friendly.

"I don't know. It just died on me. The engine started grinding and then I lost power and coasted to a stop." I pick up my phone. "And there's no cell service out here." Not that I can actually afford to call for help.

"Yeah, sorry. You won't get a signal out here. Closer to town, yes, but not here. This late at night, the auto repair center is closed, but I can radio the owner and see if he can come out here anyway and tow you to his shop."

I wince, thinking about the late hour. But more importantly, how much will a tow cost? "You don't think he'll mind?"

"Nah. He's a night owl." The man presses a button on the radio clipped to his shoulder.

There's a loud squawk, and then a woman answers. "Whatcha need, Sheriff?"

"Hey, Regina. I'm out on the state route about five miles north of Bryce, with a young lady whose car is broken down on the side of the road. Would you see if you can reach Micah and ask him to come tow her to his shop?"

"Will do," the woman says. "Just a sec."

The sheriff gazes down at me. "While we're waiting, can I please see your license, registration, and proof of insurance?"

"Sure." My hands are shaking as I reach into my purse for my wallet. Cops make me nervous. I hand him my driver's license.

He shines his light on it. "You're from Denver, huh?"

"Yes, sir."

"What brings you all the way out here in the middle of the night?"

"I prefer traveling at night. Less traffic. I'm headed to Estes Park on a sight-seeing trip."

He frowns. "Alone?"

"Yes, sir."

"How about that registration and proof of insurance?"

"Oh, right." I pull a folded sheet of paper out of the glove box and hand it to him. Then I grab my phone and show him my digital insurance card.

He looks over my insurance card and nods. "Thanks. I'll be right back."

I know it's protocol for him to call in my license and vehicle registration to make sure I don't have any outstanding warrants, but still it makes me nervous. I keep reminding myself to calm down—*I* haven't broken any laws. In fact, I'm running away from people who *want* me to break the law.

After a few minutes, the sheriff returns to my window and hands me my documents. "Tow truck's on its way. We'll have you off this road and somewhere safe in no time."

"Did they happen to mention how much the tow costs?" I'm betting I don't have enough to cover it. In fact, I'm sure I don't.

The sheriff studies me a moment. "I'm afraid not. But don't worry. We'll work something out. For now, just hang tight while we wait."

My jaw tightens. Yeah, I'm sure *we* can work something out. If not with him, then with the tow truck driver, I'll bet.

*How much does a tow cost? A blow job? Two?*

This is what they mean when they talk about jumping from the frying pan into the fire. My pulse picks up again. I did not run away from Ricky and his drug dealer just to end up a victim to small-town corruption.

The sheriff goes back to his SUV to wait for the tow truck, leaving me alone to worry about how I'm going to get out of this. I can't afford a tow, but I can't sit out here on the highway forever. And I have no money for repairs. What if it's not something simple? What then?

My mind churns through a variety of scenarios, everything from a minor repair to something major. Whatever the problem is, I'll figure it out. I have to. And then I'll get back on the road. The sooner I put Denver a thousand miles behind me, the better.

Not ten minutes later, bright lights practically blind me as a monster tow truck pulls up alongside my car. I catch sight of the logo—*Jackson's Auto Repair*.

The driver's window comes down, and I glimpse a tall, dark-haired man seated behind the wheel. I can hardly make him out as he's sitting in the shadows.

The sheriff comes to stand between our two vehicles. "Thanks for coming out so late, Micah," he says to the driver. "I owe you one."

"It's no problem." The man's voice is deep. "Just let me get this thing turned around." He drives forward a short distance, performs an impressive multi-point turn, and then pulls up on the shoulder in front of me. The tow truck beeps loudly as it backs up until there's just a few feet between us.

The driver's door opens, and a tall man with a long black braid jumps down from the cab. "Evenin', Sheriff," he says as he approaches.

The sheriff shakes his hand. "Sorry to bother you so late, but as you can see—"

"It's fine. I was still up." The man heads toward my open window and stops, his hands on his hips. He's dressed in blue jeans and a navy blue sweatshirt and is holding a heavy-duty black flashlight.

I gaze up at him—at his high cheekbones, warm brown skin, and dark eyes. There's a thin, brown leather choker around his neck holding a single turquoise pendant. *Native American.*

"Mind popping the hood for me, miss?" he asks.

I reach down to release the latch, and the man—Micah—lifts the hood and peers down at the engine, using his high-powered flashlight to see by. The sheriff moves to stand beside him, and I can hear the two men chatting.

"Try starting the engine," Micah calls to me.

I turn the key, and the engine starts right up. Surely that's a good sign.

"Well, it's not the battery," Micah says. "I was hoping for something easy."

The two men step away from the car.

"Try pulling forward a few inches," Micah says.

I put the car in drive and press lightly on the gas pedal. Just like before, the engine revs, but the car doesn't move.

The tow truck driver returns to my window. "Did you try to move forward?"

"Yes." I try again. "Nothing."

He frowns as he looks toward the sheriff. "I'll tow it to

my shop and do a thorough inspection in the morning. There's not much I can do out here in the dark."

The sheriff opens my door. "Step on out, miss, while Micah hooks your car up to the truck."

I grab my phone and purse and step out onto the road. The temperature has dropped, and I'm not dressed for it. A breeze blows right through my jean jacket, and I shiver.

Two things strike me at once. This guy is big—the tow truck driver. I'm guessing he's a couple inches over six feet tall, and he's built. Like really muscular. He's also younger than I expected. I was expecting some beer-bellied, middle-aged old guy, but no. He's probably not even thirty yet. I glance up into his face and my breath is knocked right out of me. He's the most strikingly handsome man I've seen in person.

Micah holds out his hand and gazes down at me expectantly. "Your key?" he finally asks when I stand there staring at him like an idiot.

"Oh, right. Sorry." Flustered, I hand him my key chain.

He nods toward the cab of his truck. "If you like, you can climb up into the front passenger seat and wait while I hook up your car. The heat's on. You'll be warmer in there."

"I can't stay in my car?" I really don't like the idea of

climbing into a complete stranger's truck.

He shakes his head. "Sorry, no. It's not safe."

"It's okay, Robyn," the sheriff says. "I'll follow you to the auto shop. Or, if you prefer, you can ride in my vehicle."

I'm wondering how he knows my name, but then I remember he looked at my driver's license.

Do I ride with the sheriff or with the tow truck driver? I look from one man to the other. Which is the lesser of two evils? They're both complete strangers, but I'm out here on a deserted road in the middle of the night. I can't afford to be too picky. Not unless I want to walk in the dark and freeze my ass off.

"I'll make it easy on you," the tow truck driver says, as if he can read my mind. He nods to the SUV. "Ride with Chris."

*Chris?*

Frowning, I glance at the sheriff. His name tag says *C. Nelson*. Oh. Chris. Apparently these two know each other pretty well if he's calling the sheriff by his first name.

As I shiver violently, the sheriff motions to his vehicle. "Come on. Let's get you out of this night air. Have you got a heavier coat in your car?"

"No. Just this."

The sheriff motions toward his vehicle. "Shall we?"

I follow him, and he opens the rear passenger door for me. His engine's still running, and the heat is on. I hear intermittent voices coming over his radio.

"I'm sorry to be a bother," I say as he slips into the driver's seat.

"It's no trouble." He meets my gaze in the rear view mirror. "That's what I'm here for. To help folks. Protect and serve." He pauses a moment before he adds, "Micah may look intimidating, but trust me, he's one of the good guys."

"I didn't mean to imply—"

"I know. And it's okay. Trust me, we get it. You can't be too careful these days, can you?"

It's not long before the tow truck pulls away, taking my car with it. We follow in the SUV. It's about a 10-minute drive until we reach a small town—Bryce, Colorado, according to the welcome sign, population 812. Another mile down the road, the tow truck pulls into an auto repair shop on the left-hand side of the road.

There are several buildings, the biggest one in the center, and two smaller ones alongside it. The place is dark, which is to be expected. The parking lot is lit up by streetlights.

Micah pulls close to one of the garage bay doors and lowers my car to the ground.

The sheriff parks in front of the shop and turns to face me. "It's too late for Micah to do anything with your car tonight. What do you want to—"

I jump at the sound of knuckles rapping on the sheriff's window. He rolls it down.

"What do you want to do with her tonight?" Micah asks as he nods in my direction. "The motel's closed."

The two men eye each other.

The sheriff says, "I could drive over there and see if I can get them to open up."

I can't afford a motel. I don't even have enough to pay for the tow. I lean forward and peer out the driver's window. "That's okay. I can sleep in my car."

Micah glances at me, and then back at the sheriff, and shakes his head. "Don't bother with the motel. She can sleep in my office." He opens my door. "There's a comfortable sofa in there, plus a kitchen and a bathroom with a shower. You'll have everything you need."

My heart starts pounding. But when I look at the sheriff, he nods to me, as if to say, *It's okay. It's safe.*

Micah stands by my door patiently, waiting for me to

make up my mind.

Beggars can't be choosers, so I step out of the SUV. "Thanks for the ride," I tell the sheriff.

He gives me a salute. "No problem, young lady. Try to get some sleep. I'll come back to check on you in the morning." And then he pulls out of the parking lot and turns left, his tail lights quickly disappearing from sight, leaving me alone with Micah.

I shudder visibly, but whether it's from the cold or from nerves, I don't know.

Micah gestures toward the big, darkened building. "Come on. I'll show you where you can sleep tonight."

"I really don't mind sleeping in my car."

He frowns. "I'm not about to let you sleep out here. The office is heated. You'll be comfortable—" He pauses. "I'm sorry, I didn't catch your name."

"It's Robyn, with a *y*. Robyn O'Neil."

"Look, *Robyn with a y*, in case you haven't noticed, it's late and it's cold out. You need a warm, safe place to sleep tonight." He sighs. "I promise you I'm not a serial killer. I'm just an auto mechanic."

As he cracks a smile, I feel my guard dropping. I'm not getting any red flag vibes from Micah. He seems like a decent guy. And, more importantly, I don't think the sheriff would have left me here alone with this guy if there was a chance he might murder me in my sleep. "I guess I don't have any other option. So, thanks."

"No problem," he says as he offers me my key chain. "Is there anything you need to get out of your car?"

I take it. "Yes, my backpack." I grab my backpack from the back seat, lock up my car, and follow Micah inside the auto shop.

He turns on a desk lamp. "This is the front office. My office is this way."

I follow him into a room off the main office. He switches on a light, revealing a comfortable space. There's a computer desk and chair at the back of the room. Up front is a long, black leather sofa with a coffee table and two end tables holding lamps. On the walls are a variety of framed photographs, some landscapes and some family shots.

There's one of him, much younger, standing next to a stunning woman with dark eyes and a long black braid, an older white guy, and an even older white couple.

He notices me looking at the photo. "That's my sister, Ruth, and me with our dad and grandparents."

"Is your dad around?"

"He lives in Vancouver. He's an architect, and he travels a lot for work."

"And your mom?"

"She died when I was a toddler."

I feel a stabbing pain in my chest. We both lost our moms way too early.

Micah points to a photo on his desk. It's a much younger version of his father standing with his arm around a beautiful, young Native American woman with long black hair in a braid. "My parents shortly after they got married."

"She's beautiful."

He nods. "Yeah. Ruth looks so much like her."

"And this one?" I point to a framed photo on the wall of him standing beside a helicopter, dressed in military garb.

"I served as a medevac pilot in the Army. That's me in Afghanistan."

Micah opens up a metal cabinet and pulls out a stack of bedding and a pillow. "These are clean," he says. "In case you were wondering."

I smile. "Thanks."

He lays the bedding and pillow on the coffee table and proceeds to make up the bed. He even puts a fresh pillowcase on the pillow before he props it against one arm of the sofa. "If you get cold, there's an extra blanket in the cabinet." He moves toward the door, motioning for me to follow. "Come. The bathroom's right next door, and there's a kitchen off the front office with plenty of snacks and drinks. Help yourself to anything you want."

"Thanks."

When we return to his office, he points to the doorknob. "There's a lock on the door. Feel free to use it. I want you to feel comfortable."

The knot in my stomach loosens a bit more. "Thanks."

He grabs a piece of paper off his desk and jots something down. "Here's my number. Call or text if you need anything tonight. I won't be far."

"If you don't mind me asking, where do you live?"

"I have a cabin out back behind the auto shop. Do you have everything you need?"

"Yes, thanks."

"Okay. Call me if you need anything. When I leave, I'll set the security alarm. No one can enter the building without you knowing it. I'll see you in the morning. I'm usually the first one here, but I do have three employees, so don't freak out if someone gets in before me."

And then he's gone, leaving me alone in a silent, unfamiliar space.

I make a beeline for the bathroom because my bladder's about to burst. I wash my hands afterward and then go looking around in the kitchen. It's surprisingly just like a home kitchen, with home appliances and a fully-stocked refrigerator. I grab a glass from an overhead cupboard and pour myself a glass of water. I down the entire thing, and I'm still so thirsty I end up drinking a second glass. Now I'll surely have to pee again in the night, but it can't be helped.

I find a box of peanut butter crackers and devour one of the packages, and then I eat a banana.

After a quick stop in the bathroom to wash my face and brush my teeth, I return to Micah's office and lock myself in. I plug my phone in to charge and check my messages. There are ten new messages from Ricky, each one more disturbing than the one before. They become downright threatening. He sounds desperate, scared even. Drugs and desperation are a bad combination. I've seen it destroy too many people.

I don't bother replying to any of his messages. I keep my phone on *do not disturb* and let it charge.

Micah was right when he said the sofa was comfortable. I sink into the well-worn cushions with a sigh and will my body to relax.

*I'm okay.*

*I'm in a safe place.*

And most importantly, no one knows where I am.

I close my eyes and count slowly to twenty—something that always helps me unwind. I don't even make it to ten before I lose track and my thoughts start drifting.

My mom always told me things always look brighter in the morning. My throat tightens, like it always does when I think of her. The last time I saw her alive, she was getting dressed up to go on a date night with my dad. He was going to take her out for dinner, and then they were going to see a movie. I was ten. I put myself to bed before they got home late that night. When I woke up, she was dead on the living room floor of a drug overdose. My dad must have panicked, because he was nowhere to be found. Two days later, he was arrested and charged with drug trafficking. He was the one who'd given her the cocaine tainted with fentanyl.

As an orphan, with no other family, I'd been placed in the foster care system. And that's where I met Ricky. Ricky and Robyn. I used to pretend we were twins. We were the same age, the same height. We both had blue eyes. His hair was blond, though, and mine is auburn. He protected me. I helped him with his school work. We were a team. And finally, I had family again.

And now, even that's been taken from me.

The last thing I do is send text messages to my bosses back home, explaining that I had to leave town suddenly and that I don't plan on returning.

I pull the bedding up to my chin and snuggle into the pillow. Tomorrow's another day, and I'll face whatever challenges come my way then.

## 3

## *Micah*

I'm reluctant to leave Robyn alone in the shop. She's obviously stressed out, scared even. I text Chris.

**Me: Robyn is settled for the night in my office.**

**Chris: Thanks for the update. I've got a bad feeling. Keep an eye out.**

**Me: Will do. What kind of bad feeling?**

**Chris: She's scared. Maybe she ran away from something?**

After setting the alarm and locking up the shop, I

head out back to my cabin. It's located about two hundred yards behind the shop, just inside the woods that make up the majority of my 20-acre property. I live in a small, one-room log cabin my grandfather built with his own hands back in the 1930s. It's nestled in the trees, half hidden from sight. It's quiet and peaceful back here, just how I like it.

I let myself in and flip on a couple of lights so I can see what I'm doing when I stoke the wood stove for the night. It's nearly 2 AM now, and I'm pretty wiped, so I head straight for the bathroom to get ready for bed. It looks like I'll be lucky to manage four or five hours of sleep before I'm back at work. I definitely want to make sure I get in before the others do. I don't want Robyn or my employees to be startled.

After stripping down to my boxer briefs, I climb into bed. Worn out after a long day, I expect to fall asleep as soon as my head hits my pillow. But I don't. Twenty minutes later, I'm still staring at the wooden rafters overhead.

*That girl.* She's stunning.

She's tall for a girl, probably five-eight, with long, wavy auburn hair and the biggest blue eyes I've ever seen. She has a pretty, round face, her pale cheeks dotted with tiny freckles. And her mouth! She has a wide, pouty mouth that gives a man dreams.

The moment I first laid eyes on her, my heart stuttered and my lungs seized up. My skin drew tight as heat raced through me.

It's just my luck the most attractive girl I've ever laid eyes on is passing through my town. But I'm sure Bryce will become a distant speck in her rearview mirror the minute I get her car fixed.

*Robyn with a y.*

I roll over and try to get comfortable, but it's hard to relax when I know she's sleeping in my office just two hundred yards away. On *my* sofa. On a sofa I've slept on a hundred times before.

I just hope there's nothing seriously wrong with her car, because the sooner she's gone from here, the better it will be for my sanity.

\*\*\*

When my alarm goes off at six-thirty, I haul ass out of bed, take a quick shower, dress, and head across the yard into the shop. I'm eager to check on Robyn. I also want to get in before Margie, my office manager, and Pete and

Tony, mechanics who work for me. I want to avoid any unwelcome surprises.

I let myself in through the back door of the shop and turn off the alarm. Then I switch on the lights in the garage before heading to the office, which is still quiet and dark. The front office is Margie's domain. She's not in yet, but she will be any minute. Like me, she's an early bird.

I turn on the lights before heading to the kitchen to put on a pot of coffee. Rule number one around this place—whoever gets in first puts on the coffee.

While the coffee pot's doing its thing, I knock on my office door. "Robyn? It's Micah. Are you awake?"

I hear the lock disengage, and then the door opens.

"Good morning," she says, her voice groggy from sleep.

It looks like she slept in her clothes last night, but I don't blame her. She probably felt a bit uncomfortable undressing in a strange place. Her hair is a mess, the long strands tangled around her shoulders. Obviously, she just rolled out of bed, and the thought makes my gut tighten.

I try not to stare, but it's hard. The girl is gorgeous. "I'm sorry if I woke you. My employees will be arriving soon, and I didn't want them to startle you."

She shakes her head. "It's okay. I need to be up."

"Do you drink coffee?"

Her pretty blue eyes perk up at that. "Yes, please. I would kill for a cup."

I chuckle. "Well, there's no need for any killing. It'll be ready soon." As the words come out of my mouth, the front door opens. "That's Margie, my office manager." I nod toward the office. "When you're ready, why don't you come say hi?"

I leave Robyn to get herself ready and head out to update Margie on last night's events.

Margie McMahon was my high school algebra teacher. She retired from teaching years ago, but she hated sitting around at home so she came to work for me. She's 76 years old, with short silver hair and shrewd brown eyes. She keeps this place running like a well-oiled machine, pardon the pun. She says keeping a tight rein on the three of us beats trying to motivate teenagers to do their math homework.

I fill her in on Robyn's situation and the fact that she spent the night in my office.

Margie's eyes widen. "Really? Do I know her?"

"You do not," I say. "She's from out of town, just passing through."

Right on cue, Robyn walks into the front room, her hair freshly combed and pulled back into a ponytail. It looks like she's changed her clothes.

"Well, hello there, young lady," Margie says as she beams at Robyn. "Aren't you a sight for sore eyes." She winks at me. "Isn't that right, Micah?"

Robyn's pale cheeks flush pink. "Hello."

"Don't mind Margie," I say. "She has no filter."

Margie smiles at Robyn. "Honey, at my age, there's no need for a filter. I say what I mean, and I mean what I say."

"Margie, this is Robyn, with a y," I say. "Robyn, this is Margie, my former high school algebra teacher." I point out the big front window. "That's Robyn's Civic out front. It died on her last night on the highway just north of town. I towed it here, and I'm going to take a look under the hood this morning and see what the problem is."

"You've come to the right place, Robyn," Margie says. "These boys can fix anything."

"Hopefully it's nothing serious," I say. "The coffee should be ready soon. Help yourself."

The front door opens and in walks Pete wearing dark-blue coveralls that are permanently stained with automotive grease. He's the youngest of the three of us mechanics. "Coffee," he growls.

"Good morning to you, too, sunshine," Margie says as she points to the kitchen. "It's ready."

Pete starts across the room, but when he notices Robyn, he stops dead in his tracks and does a double-take. "Hello!" His eyes widen. "Who do we have here?"

Before I can answer, Tony walks in behind him, his black hair still damp from a shower. "Good morning, everyone!" He spots Robyn immediately. "Whoa."

They act like they've never seen a woman before. I refrain from rolling my eyes. "Guys, this is Robyn. That's her car out in the lot. It died on her last night out on the highway. Robyn, this is Pete, and this is Tony. Both mechanics."

"What's wrong with her car?" Tony asks.

"Not sure yet. I'm about to find out."

"I'll take a look," Pete says.

I'm not surprised he'd volunteer. Tony has a girlfriend, but Pete doesn't. And not for lack of trying.

"You can start by helping me roll it into the garage."

While he sits behind the wheel, with the car in neutral, I push it inside. Whatever's wrong with it, I'm hoping it's a quick repair. But there's no telling with these older models. Her car is thirty years old. Hell, it's two years older than I am.

Once I have the car in the garage, I head back into the office for coffee. Robyn is seated on the sofa in the front office sipping hers.

"Has Robyn had breakfast yet?" Margie asks me as she sits at her desk.

"She just woke up," I point out. "There hasn't been time for breakfast."

"Where are your manners, Micah? You need to get that poor girl something to eat. The car can wait an hour. Take her to Jenny's."

"I'll take her," Pete offers, a hopeful expression on his face. He's barely twenty, and I think he's in love.

"That's all right," I say, feeling a bit protective of the girl, as if she's my personal responsibility. "I'll take her."

Pete looks disappointed. "Really, I don't mind." He pats his flat belly. "I could use one of Jenny's breakfast specials myself."

"Pete, if you want to be useful, go check out her car. The sooner we get it fixed, the sooner she can be on her way. I'm sure she's got someplace she needs to be."

Pete frowns. "So soon?"

"Yes," I say. "That soon."

Robyn's been watching the conversation with great interest. "I'll just be a minute," she says, pointing behind her at the bathroom.

"Take your time," I tell her.

Once she's out of sight, I level my gaze on Pete, who's following her with his gaze. "Isn't there something you should be doing?"

Muttering under his breath, he disappears through the door leading to the service area.

Margie snickers. "You can't blame him, Micah. It's not every day a pretty girl like that shows up out of nowhere. Of course he's interested."

"She's just passing through, Margie. She'll be gone before the end of the day."

"That's a shame if you ask me." She turns in her seat to face her computer screen. "We could use a little more excitement around here."

I head for the front door. "Tell Robyn I'll be waiting for her outside in my truck."

I climb up into the cab of my black Ford 350 and start the engine. Five minutes later, when Robyn comes outside, she glances around the front lot, looking for me. She waves when she spots me and heads my way.

It's only two miles to downtown Bryce, all four blocks of it. *Jenny's Diner* is right in the middle of town, sandwiched between my sister Ruth's tavern on the left and Maggie Emerson's grocery store on the right. Ruth, Jenny, and Maggie are thick as thieves. Always have been.

This early on a Monday morning, traffic is light.

I luck out and find a parking spot right in front of the diner. We hop out of the truck and head inside, and I open the door for Robyn. As the bell overhead announces our arrival, everyone in the dining room turns to look at us. It's a little after seven-thirty now, and the breakfast crowd is in full swing.

"Micah! What a pleasant surprise!" Jenny Lopez, owner of this fine establishment, rushes forward.

Jenny and I went to school together, along with Chris Nelson, the sheriff. The three of us were inseparable all throughout our school years. We're still good friends.

Jenny's all smiles as she gives Robyn the once-over. "Who's your friend?" she asks, curiosity sparking in her dark brown eyes.

"Jenny, this is Robyn. With a *y*. Robyn, this is Jenny. She owns the diner."

Robyn grins. "Yeah, I figured that. The name out front gives it away."

Jenny's smile brightens. "Ooh, I like her already." She winks at me. Then, to Robyn, she says, "It's nice to meet you, Robyn. Come right in." Jenny directs us to a table for two near the front windows. "Have a seat." She sets two menus on the table before stepping away to grab a coffee pot. "Coffee?" she asks when she returns.

"Yes, please," Robyn says.

She doesn't even bother to ask me.

Jenny turns over the mugs in front of us and pours the coffee.

I reach for my cup and take a sip. "Thanks, Jenny. I'll have the breakfast special with links and toast."

Jenny nods, not bothering to write anything down. I've been eating the same thing here for breakfast for years. She turns to Robyn. "And for you, sweetie?"

Robyn's eyes flash to me for a moment, then back to Jenny. "Just coffee, thanks."

Jenny frowns. "You sure you don't want anything to eat?"

"I'm sure," she says.

"You need to eat something," I say to Robyn.

She shakes her head. "I'm fine, really."

I know she hasn't eaten anything yet today. I also notice she's surreptitiously eyeing the menu. "Do you have any food allergies?" I ask her.

Robyn looks at me quizzically. "No. Why?"

"Are you on any special diet? Like, are you a vegetarian or a vegan?"

She chuckles. "No. Why?"

I glance at Jenny. "She'll have the breakfast special, too."

Robyn shakes her head adamantly. "No. I—"

"You need to eat something," I say.

Robyn sighs, her shoulders dropping. "Fine. I'll have some toast, then." She nods to Jenny. "With butter, please. And strawberry jam, if you have it."

When Jenny turns her gaze to me, I repeat, "*Two* breakfast specials."

"Don't waste your breath arguing with him, hon," Jenny tells Robyn. "He's as stubborn as a mule. Now, how do you like your eggs?"

Robyn scowls at me. "Scrambled," she bites out.

"Bacon or sausage?" Jenny asks her.

"Bacon."

"Toast or pancakes?"

Robyn glances up at Jenny, her expression instantly transformed. "Did you say pancakes?"

Jenny nods. "With real maple syrup."

"I'll have the pancakes." Robyn's tone softens. "Thank you."

Jenny leaves to put in our order.

Robyn's expression tightens as she crosses her arms over her chest. "You don't need to order for me."

"Fine. Then stop pretending you're not hungry, when I know you are. And don't take it out on Jenny." I take a sip of my coffee. "When was the last time you had a decent meal?"

"Not that it's any of your business, but I only have sixty dollars *to my name*."

"Don't sweat it. Breakfast is on me. I can spare eight bucks."

"You don't get it. I don't have enough money for the tow last night, let alone for any repairs. I—"

"It's okay. We'll work something out."

Her eyes narrow on me. "And just what does that mean?"

I sigh. I'm trying to be nice here, but all I'm doing is pissing her off. That was never my intention. "It means we'll work something out."

"Sure we will." Her voice hardens. "Where I come from, nobody does anything for free. There's a price for everything, and there are some prices I refuse to pay."

She leans back in her seat with a huff.

I finally catch her meaning and any frustration I might have felt vanishes. "Are you implying that I would try to take advantage of you?"

She raises an eyebrow as if to say *duh*.

"Well, you're wrong," I say. "Dead wrong."

We both sit there for a few long minutes not looking at each other. She's annoyed at me for making her order food, and now I'm aggravated because she thinks I would ever take advantage of her. Before I can figure out how to resolve our impasse, Jenny returns with our food.

She sets our plates in front of us. "Let me know if you need anything else."

"Thanks," we say in unison.

Robyn and I eat in silence, still avoiding eye contact. But my irritation with her evaporates when I notice how she's wolfing down her food—first the eggs, then the bacon and hash browns. She saves the pancakes for last, slathering them with butter and warm maple syrup. When she takes her first bite, she closes her eyes as if she's relishing the taste.

Chris is right to be concerned. She's not only broke, *she's hungry*. The realization makes my chest ache.

*Robyn with a y… what's your story?*

# 4

## *Robyn*

It's hard to sit across the table from Micah and not stare at him. He's ridiculously handsome, his skin a shade of light warm brown, his eyes dark as night. He has a strong jaw and high cheekbones. And that long, silky black hair! A lot of women would kill for hair like that.

I'm dying to ask him more about his background. Obviously he's Native American. Would it be rude of me to ask which tribe?

At face value, he seems like a truly nice guy, but I've been burned often enough that I've learned not to trust anyone—well, except for Ricky. Or, I used to trust him. Not any more, though.

I save my pancakes for last—they're dessert as far as I'm concerned. I smother them in butter and maple syrup and try not to shovel them into my mouth, but it's hard. I'm not used to eating this much food at once. I'm so full, my stomach feels like it's about to burst, but there's no way I'm missing out on these pancakes. I'm not going to waste one bite because I don't know when I'll get food like this again. My typical breakfast is a bowl of cold cereal.

I usually only have time to grab something quick between jobs—a cold sandwich or yogurt or fruit. I'm embarrassed to admit I never learned how to cook. My mom died before she could teach me, and my foster parents didn't care.

As Micah finishes the last of his coffee, he glances down at my empty plate. I didn't leave a crumb. It was that good.

"I see you like pancakes," he says with a hint of a smile.

I think he's trying not to gloat. Wiping my mouth on a napkin, I nod. "Guilty."

"Shall we head back to the shop and see what the guys have found?" he asks. "Hopefully they've got some good news for us."

*Us.* I take one last sip of my coffee. "Yeah, let's go."

Micah stands, pulls his wallet out of his back pocket, and drops a twenty and a ten on the table. Twenty bucks for the food and a ten-dollar tip. Generous.

As I stand, Jenny calls, "Have a good day, guys!" from behind the counter.

I wave to her before we reach the door. Once outside, we climb into Micah's pickup, and we're on our way back to his shop.

The moment we pull into the lot, the two mechanics rush out to meet us.

"Well?" Micah asks them as he rolls down his window.

The two mechanics look at each other, neither one of them seeming happy.

Finally the younger one, Pete, says, "I'm sorry to be the bearer of bad news, but it's her transmission. It's totally shot, Micah. The gear teeth are snapped off and the bearings are destroyed."

Micah turns to me. Clearly, based on his tight expression, this is *really* bad news. My stomach drops.

He sighs. "I'm sorry, Robyn."

"So, what does this mean?" I ask. "Can you fix it?"

Micah frowns. "Unfortunately, it's past fixing. It would have to be replaced."

"She might as well total it," Pete says. "A rebuilt transmission would cost as much as the vehicle is worth."

"Total it? No!" They'd never understand how much this vehicle means to me. I turn to Micah. "Can you fix it?"

"Yes, of course I can fix it," he says. "I'll have to find a suitable replacement and get it shipped here. But yes, I can fix it."

I'm flooded with relief. It would kill me to get rid of this car.

Pete winces. "A decent rebuilt transmission is going to cost around fifteen hundred, plus installation. You're probably looking at two grand."

My gaze snaps to Micah, who's scowling at Pete for blabbing that part of the bad news. "Two grand?" My relief is short-lived.

"With labor included, yeah," he says. "I'm afraid so."

My stomach sinks. "I don't have that kind of money."

Pete shrugs. "You'd be better off spending that kind of money to get yourself something from this century."

"No." Pain knifes through me. Even though this isn't

her actual car, it's the same make and model, even the same gray color. I remember that vehicle, remember riding in the car with her, like it was yesterday. This car is the only physical connection I have to my mom. "I don't care how much it costs to fix. I'm keeping it."

Pete and Tony eye each other, and although they don't say it out loud, I know they think I'm nuts.

"It has a lot of sentimental value," I say.

I glance past the guys to my car, which is sitting in the shop, its hood propped up. My mind is racing. My car is dead, so I have no transportation. No place to stay. And no money for a motel.

"Is there someone you can call?" Tony asks. "Someone you can borrow the money from?"

I shake my head. "No. No one."

Inside, I'm panicking. I'm stuck here. Trapped. So much for my escape plan. I didn't even make it out of Colorado. I doubt Ricky or his drug dealer boss could find me here—this place is too far off the beaten path. But I'm only an hour-and-a-half from Denver, and that's too close for comfort.

I glance at Micah, who looks just as unhappy about the news as I am. "I don't have the money," I say. *Duh.* He already knows I'm broke.

"Robyn—"

I can't bear to hear the pity in his voice, so I hop out of the truck and start walking. I've got to figure this out, fast.

"Robyn, wait!" he calls. "Where are you going?"

"To find a job!"

When I reach the road, I turn left, heading south, in the direction we just came. Hopefully I can find a job in town.

I need to earn two thousand dollars as quickly as I can. More, actually, as I owe Micah for the tow. My freedom, maybe even my life, depends on it.

* * *

It's a two-mile walk back to the little rinky-dink downtown where we had breakfast. I figure I'll start there. I remember passing several other businesses as we drove to the diner, and the downtown extends another few blocks. Hopefully someone needs help. I'm a fast learner, and I'm willing to do anything—within reason, of course.

A few cars pass me on my journey, and I get a few curious stares. I find myself holding my breath each time someone passes by as if I expect to see Ricky.

I hear the throaty roar of an engine coming up slowly behind me. When I glance back nervously, I'm relieved to see it's Micah in his pickup.

He slows to meet my pace and rolls down his window. "I'm sorry about your transmission. I was hoping it was something easy to fix."

As I keep walking along the shoulder of the road, he keeps pace with me. "Thanks. I guess it's just bad luck."

A driver comes up behind Micah and honks as he passes.

"So, what's the plan?" he asks, resting his arm on the door frame.

"I'm going to find a job."

"It's going to take you a while to earn that much money."

I shrug. "What other choice do I have?" I toss him a glance. "Don't you dare suggest some sketchy way for me to earn the money."

He chuckles. "I wasn't about to. I was going to say, I think Jenny has an opening for a server. Have you done that kind of work before?"

Suddenly, a dead weight lifts off my chest. "I've been waiting tables since I was in high school."

"Perfect. Hop in and I'll drive you down there."

I come around the front of the truck and hop up into the cab. As I buckle my seatbelt, I mentally calculate how long it will take me to save up that kind of money. With tips, I figure it'll take at least a month, probably longer if I run into additional expenses. *Damn it.* I wanted to be far from Colorado already.

"You'll need somewhere to stay in the meantime," Micah says as we pick up speed.

I turn to meet his gaze, and once again I'm struck by how handsome he is. "Maybe I could rent a room somewhere in town. That's bound to be cheaper than a motel room." But renting anything, no matter how inexpensive, is only going to prolong the length of time this is going to take.

"Or," he pauses, "you can stay in my cabin behind the auto shop. It's small, just one room, but it has everything you'd need to be comfortable."

"In your cabin? Where would you sleep?"

"In my office." He shrugs like it's no big deal. "I've done it plenty of times."

I shake my head. "I am not kicking you out of your home. You've already done so much for me."

I'm already in debt to this guy for the tow. "I haven't

forgotten I still owe you for the tow. I'll pay you for that as soon as I get my first paycheck."

He waves dismissively. "Don't worry about it. The tow's on the house."

"Micah, no. I'm not a charity case."

He's struggling not to smile. "I never said you were, Robyn."

"I can pay my own way. I owe you for the tow, plus breakfast this morning. I'm good for it. I just need a little time to get the money together."

"Fine. I'll add the tow charge to your tab, but breakfast this morning was on me."

When we arrive, Micah finds an open parking spot out front. As we're approaching the diner, I spot a handwritten sign taped to the glass door, giant words in all caps.

**SERVER WANTED**
**APPLY WITHIN**

Micah points at the sign. "I told you."

Funny, I don't remember seeing that sign earlier when we stopped for breakfast.

Micah opens the door for me, and I step inside. He follows me in.

Jenny spots us from across the room and waves us up

to the counter, where we snag two available stools. She smiles at us as she pours another customer some coffee. "You two can't be hungry again already."

Micah nudges me with his elbow. "Go ahead. Ask her."

I glance at him, then at Jenny. "I saw your help wanted sign on the door. I have five years of serving experience, and I could really use a job."

Jenny's eyes widen. "Really?" Her gaze darts to Micah, then back to me. "Lucky for me then," she says. "You're hired. When can you start?"

"How about now?" I ask.

"Fantastic. Welcome to *Jenny's Diner*."

## 5

### *Micah*

I hang out at the counter while Jenny takes Robyn back to the employee break room to show her around and give her a T-shirt and an apron. I can't believe this worked out. When Robyn walked away from the shop, I had just enough time to call Jenny and ask her to put up a *help wanted* sign. I told her I'd foot the bill. I just needed her to give Robyn a job.

I'm willing to eat the cost of her rebuilt transmission, but I know Robyn won't accept a handout—hell, she had a fit over me buying her breakfast. This is the best alternative. She can earn the money she needs working for Jenny. The work won't kill her, Jenny will take good care of her, and I'll be able to keep an eye on Robyn. I know something's going on with her. I just don't know what.

Robyn's too young to be out here in the world on her own without protection. With no one looking out for her. I don't know her story, but my gut tells me she's hiding something. Or worse yet, she's running from something. Or someone. I'm not about to let anyone hurt this girl.

A heavy hand clasps my shoulder, and a familiar voice says, "Hey, man. What's up?"

My sister's boyfriend, Jack Merchant, drops down onto the empty stool beside me. Merchant, as in The Merchant of Death. That was the nickname his teammates gave him when he worked for a private black ops team that did wet work for the US government. He's retired now and working as a bartender in my sister's tavern next door.

"Gee, Jack, what brings you in here? Let me guess."

"Nothin' much." Jack grabs a discarded newspaper lying on the counter and pretends to skim the front page.

"What are you doing here?" The tavern doesn't open

for several hours, and he never comes in here without my sister. I'm guessing she sent him in here to do reconnaissance—which means Ruth has heard about Robyn.

Jack turns the page and continues to pretend he's reading the paper. "Just thought I'd stop in for coffee. What are *you* doing here? Shouldn't you be at work?"

"Are you sure my sister didn't send you here to snoop on me?"

Jack chuckles as he lays the paper down and turns another page. "Well," he drawls. "She might have caught wind of your new *lady friend*."

"She's not my *lady friend.* She's a customer. That's all."

"Right," Jack says with a long drawl.

Robyn returns to the dining room wearing a short-sleeve pink T-shirt bearing the *Jenny's Diner* logo in white letters. The form-fitting top is tucked into her jeans, which ride low on her hips. The jeans accentuate her generous curves, and the T-shirt is snug, molded to a pair of plump breasts. A white apron is tied around her waist, and her long hair is pulled back in a high ponytail.

She turns in a circle, arms outstretched. "How do I look?"

*Perfect.* "You look great."

Jack clears his throat, never once taking his eyes off

the newspaper.

Jenny comes up behind Robyn, her eyes lighting up when she sees who's sitting beside me. "Jack! What brings you in here?" She looks around, undoubtedly expecting to see my sister. "Where's Ruth?"

"Next door," he says, still focused on the paper. "Doing inventory."

"Can I get you anything?"

"Just coffee, please. I've already eaten."

"Sure thing." Jenny grabs a mug, the pot of coffee, and pours him a cup.

Robyn glances at Jack and frowns. With his dark hair and beard, swarthy complexion, and numerous tattoos, he's an intimidating sight. But the man's got a heart of gold. He risked his own life not long ago to protect my sister. I'll always have a soft spot for him for that reason alone.

"Robyn, this is Jack Merchant," I say. "He's my sister's undeserving half."

Instantly, Robyn relaxes. "Nice to meet you."

Jack chuckles as he turns the page. "Likewise."

"He's a scary son-of-a-bitch, but don't worry. My sister keeps him on a short leash."

"Funny." Jack play-punches my shoulder. "I'm this

guy's future brother-in-law. We're practically family."

Robyn looks to me for confirmation, and I nod. "Afraid so. For some crazy reason, my sister wants to keep him."

"We're all set here, Micah," Jenny says. "I'll get Robyn up to speed on how we do things." She smiles dismissively at me as if saying, *You can go now.*

Fine. I can take a hint. "See ya later, Jack." And then I meet Robyn's bright blue eyes and do my best to ignore the punch I feel. "I'll pick you up when you get off work, okay? I don't want you walking back to the auto shop."

She makes a guilty face. "Are you sure? I hate to be a bother."

"Yeah, I'm sure."

"She gets off at three," Jenny says as she comes around the counter and shoos me toward the door. "Now git back to work. We sure don't need you hovering."

I'm reluctant to leave Robyn, but when I glance back, I catch her laughing at something Jenny said to Jack. Probably something at my expense. I know Jenny will keep an eye on Robyn. I trust Jenny like I trust my own sister.

Speaking of my sister... I need to call Ruth and ask her why she sicced her attack dog on me this morning. Word sure does travel fast around here. I imagine Jenny called and told my sister I asked her to hire Robyn. That's going to lead to a lot of questions.

I walk back to my truck. Just as I'm about to back out of my parking space, the sheriff's SUV pulls in beside me. On the side of his vehicle is the familiar logo *PROTECT AND SERVE*.

*Great. More grilling.*

Chris steps out of the vehicle. He's wearing his uniform, so clearly he's on duty.

I roll down my window as he approaches.

"Micah! Just the person I wanted to see. I stopped in at the auto shop, and Margie told me you were probably here. What's the news on Robyn's car? Got it up and running yet?"

I guess word doesn't travel quite fast enough. "Unfortunately, no. Her transmission's toast."

"Oh, man." Chris shakes his head. "That's too bad. So, what's the plan? If I recall correctly, the girl's short on funds."

"The plan is, I'll rebuild her transmission, and she's going to work at Jenny's to save up the money to cover the repair."

Chris whistles. "That's going to take a while." He does the mental math. "If she works full time, with tips, it'll take her at least a month." He glances at the diner. "I thought Jenny was fully staffed."

"She is. I called in a favor."

Chris frowns at me. "What kind of *favor?*"

"Relax, Sheriff. I asked her to hire Robyn, and I told her I'd cover the cost. It won't cost Jenny a thing."

Chris nods. "All right, then. You headin' back now?"

"Yes. Apparently, I'm not needed here."

As Chris walks into the diner, I head back to the shop. I need to get busy making calls to my suppliers to find a suitable transmission.

* * *

"Find one yet?" Margie asks when she returns to the office after her lunch break.

I'm sitting at my desk, on my PC, searching the inventory of a national auto parts supply company. She walks up behind me and peers over my shoulder at my computer screen.

"Yes." I lean back in my creaky office chair. "They'll ship it out in two days. I should have it by the end of the week."

"How much?"

"A little over fifteen hundred dollars."

She whistles. "That's a lot of money for a broke twenty-something."

"It's all right. I've got it covered. She's going to earn the money working for Jenny."

Margie frowns. "Not overnight, she won't. Where's she going to stay while she's earning this money?"

"I offered her my cabin. She wasn't thrilled with the idea, but she doesn't have a lot of options."

Margie's brow furrows. "Then where are *you* going to stay? Surely not in the cabin with her."

"Of course not! I'll sleep here in my office."

Now that I've found a transmission for Robyn's car, I change into my coveralls and head into the shop to get to work. Pete's got his head buried beneath the hood of a Toyota, replacing a timing belt. Tony is changing the tires on a Ford.

"What's the word, boss?" Tony asks as he goes to grab a new tire. "Did you order the transmission?"

"Yeah. It'll be here by the end of the week."

"Where's Robyn?" Pete asks, glancing around as if he expects her to magically appear.

"She's waiting tables at Jenny's." Everyone is so damned curious about Robyn and what she's up to.

"Hey, Micah," Pete says. "Have you looked at Robyn's

tires? They're threadbare."

"No, I haven't. I was so focused on the engine, I didn't look at anything else." I walk over to her Civic and take a look at the tread on her front right tire. It is indeed threadbare. I check the other three tires and find them all worn down. "Looks like I'm changing tires."

She's not going to be happy about it, but it needs to be done. She can't drive around on those things.

I pull a set of top-quality, all-weather tires from my stock. When I raise her car on the lift and start loosening lug nuts to remove the old tires, I notice something attached to the underside of the frame. "Son of a bitch."

"What?" Tony walks over to me and peers beneath Robyn's car. "Oh, wow."

Pete's right behind him. "What is it?"

I pry a small, black magnetic box off the metal frame. It's a GPS tracking device.

Pete takes the device from me and examines it. "Holy shit. I wonder who put that there."

"Yeah, me, too," I say. I pluck the device out of Pete's grasp, drop it to the floor, and crush it under my boot heel. Now my suspicion that Robyn is in some kind of trouble takes on even more significance.

If she is running from someone, then they already

know exactly where she is. In Bryce, Colorado. At my auto repair shop.

* * *

After I finish changing the tires on Robyn's Civic, I head out back to tidy up the cabin. I change the sheets, clean the kitchen and the bathroom, sweep the floors, and take the rugs outside to beat them. I even dust. I want the place to be clean and comfortable for her.

If there's a chance someone tracked her here, she definitely needs to stay in my cabin, *with me.* I'll install a wireless security system, and I'll be on site in case we have some uninvited guests.

# 6

## Robyn

My first day working at the diner flies by. Jenny is super laid back, which is great. My last boss was a super micromanager, and that gets old real quick. I think Jenny will be a good boss. She doesn't hover, but instead lets me figure things out on my own, which works for me. I've waited tables since I was old enough to work, so I don't need hand-holding.

One of the perks of the job is that we get free meals, which is fantastic because I don't have a lot of money for groceries. I figure I can eat both breakfast and lunch at the diner. That just leaves me needing something later for dinner. I think I can afford a jar of peanut butter and a loaf of bread.

The diner's clientele is made up of half locals and half tourists, and the two groups are easy to tell apart. The locals say *hi* to Jenny and the servers when they come in. They don't bother waiting to be seated, but instead head straight for their favorite tables.

The locals know everyone working here by name, and vice versa. And most of them are dressed in blue jeans and plaid shirts. The tourists, on the other hand, stick out like sore thumbs. They're usually the ones wearing expensive brand-name outdoor clothing and fancy hiking boots.

Toward the end of the lunchtime rush hour, a really good-looking guy walks in, dressed like a cowboy with boots, hat, and all. He takes one of the booths by the front windows, leans back in his seat, and waves me over. "Over here, darlin'."

Immediately, my hackles go up.

Cara, the other server working today—a petite, curvy blonde with a nose ring—rolls her eyes as she walks past me. "Tommy Hoffman thinks he's God's gift to women, but he's loaded and he tips well."

I'm all for good tips, so I walk over to his table.

Before I can even get a word out, he asks, "What's your name, sugar?"

"It's definitely not sugar," I say, unable to help myself. I don't subscribe to the notion that customers are always right.

He grins at me, a cocky son-of-a-bitch because he's damn good-looking, and he knows it—thick blond hair that flops over his forehead, blue eyes, a tan complexion that comes from doing a lot of outdoor work. He's built like a linebacker, with not an ounce of flab on him. Of course he's wearing a plaid shirt—apparently, it's part of the dress code around here.

I give him a well-practiced smile. "My name is Robyn, and I'll be serving you today. Can I—"

"Robin? You mean, like robin redbreast?" He smirks as his gaze drops to my chest and lingers there, as if he can see right through my T-shirt.

*Like I've never heard that one before.* "Actually, no. Not like the bird. It's spelled with a *y*."

His gaze travels back up to meet mine. "Too bad. I kind of liked the idea." And then he winks at me, which is totally cringey.

I force myself to maintain a polite smile. "Can I start you off with something to drink?" I ask in the sweetest voice I can manage. After all, if he's a good tipper, I don't want to alienate him if I don't have to.

"I'll take the double-burger platter with onion rings, extra bacon and pickles, and a Coke."

I'm still smiling. "Yes, sir. Coming right up." And then I walk away to go place his order at the counter.

Jenny slips up beside me. "Is he giving you a hard time? Tommy can be a bit much sometimes."

"He's a bit creepy. He called me Robin Redbreast, like that's funny."

Jenny winces. "Sorry. Let me take his table. He won't mouth off to me because he likes to eat here. And, I'm good friends with the sheriff." She winks. "That comes in handy, believe me. If anyone gives you a hard time, just drop Chris's name. Folks around here have a lot of respect for him."

I'm relieved that I don't have to talk to the cowboy anymore. The rest of my afternoon passes without incident, and before long, it's three o'clock.

Jenny taps me on the shoulder. "Your shift is over, hon. You can change and get ready to go." She pats my back. "You did a good job today, Robyn. I'm lucky to have you."

"Thanks." I give her a smile—a genuine one. I had a good day. I even forgot all about Ricky and his drug dealer friends for a while.

Jenny nods toward the door. "Looks like your ride is here."

When I turn to look, I see Micah standing just inside the entry, next to a newspaper rack. He's leaning against the wall, his arms crossed over his broad, muscular chest. He looks… serious. Preoccupied. When he smiles at me, my chest flutters.

I point toward the hallway that leads to the employee lounge and pluck at my T-shirt, indicating that I need to go change.

He nods.

I head back to the employee lounge and walk into the women's locker room. I open my locker and grab my phone so I can check my messages. I'm not surprised to see more texts from Ricky. It's just more of the same, asking me where I am, demanding I come back.

I hang up my apron and change back into my own top. I take a moment to pee, because I haven't had time all day, and wash my hands.

I stare at myself in the bathroom mirror. My hair held up pretty well. A few strands fell loose, but it's not bad.

I'll braid it tomorrow. I contemplate brushing my hair and maybe putting on some lip gloss, but I don't want to look like I'm *trying*. For all I know, Micah has a girlfriend. Or, maybe even a wife. I know next to nothing about his personal life.

I wonder if I should maybe buy some make-up. I usually don't bother. My lashes are long, framing my eyes and making them pop. My cheeks are dusted with freckles—the bane of my existence—so I look like I already have blush on. I figure what's the point in adding more to my face? It seems complete enough.

When I head back to Micah, I stop short in my tracks. He's not alone. He's standing with a stunning woman with a long braid of straight black hair—just like Micah's. Her skin is the same shade as his—a light copper. Her eyes are so dark they appear black. She's wearing blue jeans, a red plaid flannel shirt, and well-worn leather hiking boots.

So, this is his sister. She's obviously quite a bit older than Micah.

Ruth turns to look at me, and for a long moment, we make eye contact, practically staring at each other.

Micah pushes away from the wall and motions me over.

Ruth studies me as I approach. At the last minute, her expression softens, and she smiles. "Robyn." Her voice is lovely, soft and sultry. "I'm Ruth, Micah's sister." She offers me her hand, and we shake. "It's a pleasure to meet you. I'm sorry to hear about your car, but luckily you're in good hands. Micah will get you back on the road in no time."

Nodding, I return her smile. "It's nice to meet you, too."

"I own the tavern next door," she says. "Feel free to stop by for a drink—that is, if you're twenty-one." She looks unsure. "You are twenty-one, right?"

"Twenty-three, actually."

"I'm glad to hear it," she says as she flashes her brother a look. "Please come by soon."

Ruth leaves, and Micah holds the door for me. I step out onto the sidewalk just as Ruth disappears into the business next door. I glance up at the sign over the door. *RUTH'S TAVERN.*

"I ordered your transmission," Micah says as he walks to the passenger side of his truck and opens the door for me. "It should be here in a couple of days."

Standing next to him, I'm reminded once again of how tall he is. I'm not used to guys looming over me. I'm also not used to guys opening doors for me. "I can open my own door, you know. You don't have to wait on me."

He nods. "Got it." And then he walks around to the driver's door and climbs in.

We head back to the shop, pull into the parking lot, and park in front of the office. When I open my door, I hear the sound of power tools coming from inside the garage bays.

I spot my car, which is now parked outside the building. "Wait. Something's different."

"Yeah, I put new all-weather tires on your car. The old ones were shot."

I pivot to face him, my heart thudding in my chest. "Micah! I don't have money for new tires."

He leans close, practically in my face. "Too bad," he says. "There's no point in rebuilding your transmission if you're going to drive around on threadbare tires. Those tires were an accident waiting to happen. Please don't worry about it. I gave them to you at cost." He opens his door. "You must be tired after being on your feet all day. Why don't you rest for a while in my cabin? When I get done working, I'll make us some dinner." He motions for me to follow him.

To my surprise, I readily follow Micah around the side

of the shop. I've known him for barely a day, and yet I trust him. My finely-tuned danger senses are quiet.

We walk past a patio with a picnic table, chairs, and a grill. Beyond that is a lawn, and in the distance I spot a small log cabin nestled in the trees. I have to admit it looks charming, like something out of an old western movie.

We step up onto a small, covered porch. Micah unlocks the door and motions for me to enter.

I take two steps inside and stop in my tracks. "Micah, this is gorgeous." I don't know what I was expecting, but it wasn't this. His cabin looks like something you'd see on Pinterest.

There's a huge bed straight ahead, cozy looking with lots of pillows stacked against a wooden headboard. There's a wooden bench at the foot of the bed, with an assortment of shoes and boots lined up neatly underneath. Across from the bed is a long sofa with throw pillows and a blanket tossed across the back. To the left of the bed there's a wardrobe in the corner, a window on the left-hand wall, and a brick hearth with a woodstove set inside. The floors are wood and covered with a variety of rugs in warm neutral colors.

To the right is a small but functional kitchen and a

table with four chairs. There are two doors along the back wall. I suspect one of them leads to a bathroom. The other one might lead to a laundry room or a pantry.

"This is really nice," I say as I take it all in.

He chuckles. "I can't really take credit for it. Jenny picked out the furniture and arranged everything. She's good with stuff like that."

*Jenny decorated his cabin?*

Then it dawns on me. I'm such an idiot. They're together. Of course they are. A guy this attractive would surely have a partner. My stomach drops. "I didn't realize you two were together."

His eyes widen in surprise. "Together? Who? Jenny and me? No." He shakes his head and laughs. "We've known each other since third grade. She's like a sister to me. No, she offered to help me redecorate because when she first saw it, it looked like an Army barracks. Honest."

"Oh, sorry. I just assumed." I'm tempted to ask him if he does have a girlfriend, but that would be nosy. I hardly know the guy, so his private life is none of my business.

"Well, what do you think?" he asks. "About the cabin, I mean. I'd like you to consider staying here with me instead of in my office. You can take the bed, and I'll sleep on the sofa."

The cabin is tempting beyond words, but I don't want to disrupt his private space. "It's beautiful, but I wouldn't want to intrude. I'm fine sleeping in your office."

"I'd feel better knowing you were here in the cabin, close by in case there's a problem. Especially after what I found on your car today."

"What are you talking about?"

"When I had your car up on the lift to change the tires, I found a tracking device attached to the undercarriage."

"A what!" I heard him, but I'm having trouble wrapping my mind around it.

"Someone's tracking your movements. And whoever it is knows where you are."

A chill races down my spine. "Oh, my God." My knees go weak, and I have to sit on his sofa.

"Is there someone who might do this?"

*Is there someone? Yes.* My mind races as I put two and two together. Ricky, or more likely his dealer, knows where I am. *They know.* I suddenly feel sick.

"I thought maybe you were hiding something," he says gently. "Now I'm sure of it."

As I look him in the eye, my throat tightens. "I—I don't even know where to start."

"How about at the beginning?"

I feel the blood drain from my face at the thought that someone could come here looking for me.

Micah sits on the bench at the foot of the bed and faces me. "Tell me, Robyn. Who's tracking you and why? I can't help you if I don't know what's going on."

"You can't help me. No one can."

"That's where you're wrong," he says, very matter of fact.

# 7

## Micah

Robyn seems genuinely shaken by the news there was a tracker on her car. She honestly didn't know.

"Let's start with, who put the tracker on your car?" I ask.

She meets my gaze, then looks away. "I'm not sure. It was either my roommate, Ricky, or the people he's working for. I honestly don't think it was Ricky's idea. He's not that tech savvy. If he put it on my car, he was just following orders."

"People he's working for? Who?"

"Drug dealers."

"You need to tell me what's going on, Robyn. Are you in danger?" I can tell from the flash of panic in her eyes the answer is yes.

"Last night, when my car broke down, I had just left my home in Denver. I guess you could say I ran away."

"Why?"

She sighs. "I share—shared—an apartment with a long-time friend, Ricky. He's actually more like a brother to me. We grew up together in foster care. When we aged out of the system at the same time, we decided to stick together. He's an orphan, like me, and it just made sense. We lived in a group home for young adults for a while, until we'd saved up enough money to get an apartment together. Between the two of us, we were working four jobs just to stay afloat."

She stands and starts pacing, obviously too agitated to stay in one place. "Lately, I'd begun to suspect that Ricky was doing drugs. He'd started acting strange, erratic, and I recognized the signs." She pauses to face me. "I don't touch the stuff."

I keep quiet, letting her tell her story in her own time.

"Both my parents were drug addicts, so I'm familiar with the signs. My mom OD'd after taking cocaine tainted with fentanyl when I was ten, and my father went to prison for dealing. He's the one who gave her the cocaine, although I believe him when he said he didn't know it was tainted. He loved her. He never would have hurt her intentionally."

She's quiet for a moment as a profound sadness descends on her, nearly transforming her right in front of me. The light is gone from her eyes. In its place are sorrow and pain. So much pain.

"You didn't have any other family to take you in?" I ask.

"No one. I became a ward of the state and ended up in foster care." Her eyes tear up, but she wipes them as if she's embarrassed to show emotion.

"I found out last night that not only is Ricky using drugs, but he started working for a local dealer a couple of weeks ago. The guy's name is Verne. That's all I know. I've never even met him, but he knows about me thanks to Ricky. Ricky promised Verne I would deliver a shipment of meth to Seattle. Of course I never agreed to any such thing. I don't want anything to do with drugs. They're the reason my family was destroyed.

"Ricky started panicking when I refused to act as a drug mule. He'd already promised Verne I would. I think Ricky was afraid of what Verne would do when he found out I wanted no part in it.

"So I ran. I grabbed my backpack and a few belongings, and I hit the road. I was planning to go south to Arizona. Someplace far away from Denver, where I could start over. Obviously, I didn't get very far."

"And now they know where you are. Do you think they'll come after you?"

Robyn shrugs. "I guess it depends on how angry Verne is. Ricky said the guy wouldn't take no for an answer." She swallows hard. "I think the real problem is that Ricky told me everything—their plans, the quantity to be delivered, even the destination in Seattle."

"And the dealer may decide you know too much."

She nods. "That's what I'm afraid of."

"Robyn, we need to assume the worst—that they might come after you. I need to let Chris know. He and his deputies can be on the lookout for unfamiliar vehicles in the area. Have you spoken to Ricky since you've been here?"

"Not directly, no. He's been texting me, each message more irate than the one before, demanding that I come back to Denver."

"Is he threatening you?"

When her gaze meets mine, I can tell the answer is yes. She doesn't even need to say it. "He's not himself lately," she says. "He's under a lot of pressure, I think, and he's under the influence of drugs. Probably meth."

"Then he's dangerous."

She nods. "If I'm going to stay here in your cabin, I'll need my backpack. It's in your office."

"Wait here. I'll go grab it."

I run across the yard to the shop, grab her backpack, and return to the cabin. "Try to relax," I tell her. "Help yourself to anything in the kitchen. The bathroom's in there."

"Hand me your keychain," I say, holding out my palm.

She drops her keys in my hand, and I grab a spare key from a kitchen drawer and slip it onto her ring. "Now you can come and go as you like."

I head back to the shop so I can make some phone calls. I shut myself up in my office and call Chris first to let him know about the tracker on Robyn's car. He promises to keep an eye on the shop. And he'll put his deputies on alert.

Next I call Jack and give him the lowdown. Jack has

certain skills that would come in handy if these people do show up in Bryce. Plus, he'll pass the information on to Ruth. The more people who are vigilant, the better.

It's only four in the afternoon, so I figure I should put in some more work before I call it a day. Thank goodness the next job in the queue is an easy one—an oil change—because I'm distracted.

*Robyn's possibly in danger.*

At least she's agreed to sleep in my cabin. I can protect her better there. Even if someone tracked her car to the shop, they won't know about the cabin in back. It's not even visible from the road. They'd actually have to be snooping around to spot it.

She's spending the night in my cabin—*in my bed*—and I can't get the thought out of my mind. Not *with me*, of course. I'll be on the sofa. But I keep picturing her in my bed, her head on my pillow, my sheet and covers keeping her warm.

I can't get the image out of my head.

"Earth to Micah!" Pete yells.

Shaking free of my thoughts, I shift my attention to him. "Sorry, what?"

"I asked, where's your girlfriend?"

"She's hanging out in my cabin at the moment. And

she's not my girlfriend."

"No?" He smirks. "Then you won't mind if I ask her out?"

I can hear Tony snickering across the garage.

"Yes, I mind," I say. "She's got enough to worry about without you hitting on her. She's off limits."

"Then what's she doing in your cabin?" Pete asks.

"I told her about the tracking device, and I asked her to sleep in the cabin. She'll be safer there, and I can better protect her. You guys need to watch for anyone suspicious. If you see unfamiliar vehicles, or people, hanging around the shop, let me know. And if I'm not here, call the sheriff's office."

Pete wipes his hands on a rag. "You really think someone's looking for her?"

"It's possible. We can't take any chances. Be vigilant."

Around six, after everyone has gone home, I lock up the shop and turn on the alarm. If someone comes here and sticks his nose where it doesn't belong, I'll know about it.

The sun is setting when I walk back to the cabin. I knock first, so I don't scare her. "Robyn? It's me." And then I open the door and step inside.

She's lying on the sofa, a mini iPad in her hands. It

looks like she's reading. Flustered, she sits up and swings her feet to the floor. Her hair is up in a messy bun and she's wearing a pair of gray sweats, an oversized white sweatshirt, and a pair of pink fuzzy socks. She looks… comfortable.

"It's okay," I say, ignoring the way my pulse has picked up at the sight of her. "Make yourself at home. I want you to feel comfortable."

She grins, and I could swear she's blushing.

"What are you reading?" I ask.

She closes the case on her iPad. "A novel."

"What genre?"

She smiles. "It's a rom-com about two physicists falling in love."

"Physicists, huh? Sounds scintillating."

"Actually, it's really good." She sets her iPad on the end table. "So, what's up?"

"Can I interest you in a burger and some sweet potato fries for dinner?"

She glances down at her attire. "I'm not really dressed to go out. Besides, I already took off my bra. I'm not putting it back on for anything." She grins.

*Oh, my God.* She had to mention her bra, which of course makes me think of her breasts. My pulse races as I nod toward the kitchen. "Actually, I'm planning on cooking. I just wondered if burgers and fries sound good to you."

"Oh." Her cheeks turn pink. "You cook?"

"Yeah. My grandma made sure I learned how to fend for myself in a kitchen."

"I'd offer to help, but I know absolutely nothing about cooking. I can make macaroni and cheese from a box or a grilled cheese sandwich, but that's about it."

"You can help, if you want. I'll teach you."

She crosses the room in her fuzzy pink socks.

I look away, afraid I'll see evidence of the fact she's not wearing a bra. But on second glance, I think I'm safe. Her sweatshirt is baggy enough to camouflage her body.

I turn away so she doesn't see me smiling. "So, how are you with a knife?" When she sidles up next to me, I gesture to two large sweet potatoes lying on the kitchen counter. I turn on the oven to preheat. "How about washing those, then slicing them into fries?"

She grins. "I think I can manage that."

Standing this close to her, I notice little flecks of gold in her irises. Her lashes are long.

While she washes the potatoes, I grab a cast iron skillet and set it on the stove. I skirt around her to the fridge so I can grab a pound of ground beef.

A strong wind lashes the tree outside the kitchen window, its branches striking the glass. Robyn flinches at the noise, and for a second, I see a flash of panic in her eyes.

"It's okay," I say as I peer outside. It's just the wind. "It looks like we might have some rough weather tonight."

She busies herself with a knife and cutting board as she cuts up the potatoes. "Do you mind if I put on some music?" she asks.

"Go right ahead." I'm curious to find out her taste in music.

She brings her phone over and opens Spotify.

"I have a Bluetooth speaker you can use," I tell her, nodding to the speaker on the counter.

She pairs her phone with the speaker, and a moment later, I hear the voice of Elton John in my kitchen.

"Elton John, huh?" I ask as I make the burger patties. "He's a bit before your time, isn't he? Actually, he's before mine, too, but my sister's quite a bit older than I am. Thanks to her, I was exposed to a variety of music growing up."

"My parents played his music a lot when I was a kid." She frowns, and suddenly the sadness is back.

I step closer and gently nudge her shoulder. "I'm sorry

if I brought up painful memories."

"It's okay." She makes an effort to smile. "I want to be able to talk about them, think about them. Hearing their favorite music is bittersweet. It makes me feel closer to them."

Robyn pops the sweet potato fries into the oven, and I cook the burgers. When the food's done, we eat at the kitchen table, serenaded by the soulful sounds of Karen Carpenter singing about love.

The sadness is back in Robyn's eyes. "I remember how much they loved each other," she says as she picks up a fry. "They danced a lot in the kitchen. They'd include me, and the three of us would dance together. They were so much fun to be around. I think it destroyed my dad when my mom died. I don't think he'll ever forgive himself."

I reach across the table and squeeze her hand. "I'm sorry for your loss."

We sit in silence for a while, eating our meals. Something occurs to me. "Robyn?"

"Yes?"

"Have you ever shot a gun before? A handgun?"

"No."

"How about a lesson?"

"No, thanks. I'd rather not."

"I keep a small arsenal here in my cabin, in a locked cabinet in my closet. I'd like to teach you to shoot."

"Oh, no. I don't think that's a good idea."

"You need to be able to defend yourself in an emergency. I won't be with you every second of every day. I need to know you can protect yourself. Maybe we could start tomorrow." When she doesn't reply, I say, "Robyn?"

"I heard you."

"So, is that a yes?"

"It sounds like I don't have a choice." She stands, picks up her empty plate, and carries it to the sink. "No dishwasher?"

"No, sorry."

She shrugs. "No problem." She starts filling the sink with water. "You cooked. I'll wash."

I carry the rest of our dishes to the sink. "And I'll dry."

After we're done cleaning up after dinner, Robyn ropes me into watching an episode of *Bridgerton* on Netflix. She tries to catch me up to speed on season three but there's a lot of ground to cover. Basically, it's about single mothers trying to get their grown kids married off. It's cool how diverse the cast is. That was unexpected.

After watching two episodes, Robyn's yawning and

having trouble keeping her eyes open.

"I think it's time for bed," I say. She must be exhausted after the past twenty-four hours she's had.

She stands. "I call dibs on the bathroom."

I laugh. "Not a problem. It's all yours."

She's in the bathroom for a few minutes, and I hear the water running in the sink. The door opens, and she pops her head out, her face flushed and damp. "Um, do you have something I could sleep in? In my rush to leave home, I forgot to grab pajamas. Last night I slept in my clothes, but I didn't bring enough with me to keep doing that."

"I'm sure I can find something." I cross the room and walk into my closet, digging through my clothes. I sleep in my underwear, so I don't have a lot in the way of pajamas. I try to find something that'll be comfortable for her. I end up grabbing a pair of plaid flannel bottoms and a long-sleeve T-shirt.

"Here you go," I say as I hand her the garments. "You'll have to roll up the pant legs and the sleeves, but at least you'll be warm and comfortable."

"Thanks." She takes them from me and closes the bathroom door.

I grab a pillow, sheet, and a blanket from the closet

and make up the sofa for her. I know from personal experience that the sofa is plenty comfortable.

A few minutes later, she walks out and—*oh, man.* She looks... wow. I had no idea my clothes would look so good on her.

"Thanks. These will work great."

She heads for the sofa. "You made up the sofa. Thanks."

"Why don't you take the bed?" I ask.

"That's okay," she says as she sits down. "I'm comfortable right here."

"I don't feel right sleeping on the bed when you're roughing it."

When she shakes her head, I can see her resolve is unshakable. "Nope. I'm not kicking you out of your bed. It's either this, or—"

"Okay, fine," I say before she threatens to sleep in my office. "We'll do it your way."

# 8

## *Robyn*

After Micah takes his turn in the bathroom, he comes out dressed in a pair of gray sweats and... nothing else. My gaze locks on his torso, which is a work of art. He has abs. Like real abs. He's muscular and solid. His chest is bare, no hair.

He turns off all the lights except the one on his nightstand. I try not to stare as he peels off his sweats and tosses them aside, leaving him in a pair of black boxer shorts. His legs are long and muscular.

He sits on the edge of the bed and stares down at the floor, at his bare feet. "Robyn," his voice is quiet. "Please take the bed."

"I told you, I'm not kicking you out of your bed. I'll be fine over here."

We're at an impasse, and I can hear the frustration in his voice. I bite back a chuckle when I think his problem is that he's not used to women telling him *no*.

*There's got to be a first time for everything, buddy. Get used to it.*

With a huff, he reaches over to switch off the lamp on his nightstand, casting the room into deep shadows. He lies down and sighs heavily. Again, I struggle not to chuckle. I think our sleeping arrangements are an affront to his sense of chivalry.

We both lie in our respective beds for a good while, neither breaking the silence.

Even though I'm comfy and warm, I can't sleep. I keep thinking about Ricky, wondering what he's doing. Part of me wants to call him, just to check on him, but I know I shouldn't. He's still sending me text messages begging me to come back to Denver and go through with the delivery. And then there's the whole tracking device issue. If he had anything to do with that, he should be ashamed of himself.

Sighing, I turn over, hoping a different position will change things. I rearrange the pillow and pull the blanket closer. Nothing helps.

I hear movement coming from the bed. Micah tosses off his bedding, climbs out of bed, and walks over to me. Without a word, he yanks off my blanket, scoops me up into his arms, and carries me to the bed.

"Micah! What are you doing?"

"I can't sleep knowing you're on the sofa." He sets me down on his mattress, which is still warm from his body. "You're taking the bed, and that's that."

When I open my mouth to protest, he points his index finger at me. "I don't want to hear another word about it, Robyn."

He walks away, and a moment later, he's back with my phone, which he sets on the nightstand. "I imagine you'll need that." Then he's gone again, and I hear him settling down on the sofa.

Part of me wants to march over there and read him the riot act for manhandling me like that. I should grab my stuff and return to his office to sleep, but the thought of that tracking device stops me cold.

And another part of me is distracted by the fluttering

in my belly. *I'm in Micah's bed.*

As I roll onto my side, I detect his scent on his pillow, a combination of faint cologne, soap, and the man himself. He has no right to smell so good. And no right to be so bossy. Who does he think he is to decide where I should sleep?

"Are you warm enough?" he asks, his voice low. "I can get another blanket if you want one."

"I'm fine." Suddenly, exhaustion catches up with me. I snuggle down into the most comfortable bed I've ever slept in. The only thing that would make this moment better would be if he were sharing it with me. "Thanks."

"You're welcome."

* * *

Morning comes way too quickly. My alarm goes off when it feels like I just went to sleep. My eyes are tired and gritty, and I just want to sleep the rest of the day away. But of course I can't. I have a job to go to. With a groan, I stretch my arms and legs wide. Micah's bed is huge—it must be a king.

I glance over at the sofa just as Micah sits up. He looks as tired as I feel.

"Dibs on the bathroom," I say, with far less enthusiasm than last night. I hear him chuckling as I grab my backpack and race into the room.

"I can see how this is going to go," he calls after me. "You're a bathroom hog. That's what you are."

I wash up and dress quickly in my only other pair of clean jeans. I'll need to do laundry this evening. I should go shopping for a couple more pairs of jeans and some warm tops. I pull on a sweatshirt, clean socks, and my sneakers.

When I come out of the bathroom, Micah's in the kitchen staring at the coffee maker. He's put his sweats back on, but he's still barefoot and shirtless. I try not to ogle him, but it's hard.

"Staring at the coffee maker won't make it work faster, you know," I say.

He smiles. "Well, it sure can't hurt." He heads for the bathroom. "I hope you left me some hot water." Micah's clearly not a morning person.

I stand by the coffee maker with my cup, ready. As soon as it stops dripping, I pour a cup. I find sugar in an old-fashioned sugar bowl in a cabinet. I find French vanilla creamer in the fridge.

I'm sitting at the table, sipping my coffee when Micah

comes out of the bathroom. He disappears into his closet and reemerges a few minutes later, looking strikingly handsome in a pair of black jeans, a dark gray Henley, and a pair of black boots. He's the epitome of tall, dark, and handsome.

As I'm mid-sip, I just point at the coffee maker.

He pours himself a cup, black, and joins me at the table.

"Is there a thrift shop in town?" I ask. "I'm going to need more clothes. I didn't bring much with me. And is there a laundromat around here? I need to do a load."

He points to a door right off the kitchen. "There's a washer and dryer in there. Help yourself. As for thrift shops, yeah. There's one in town, two blocks from the diner. I can also drive you to Estes Park where there's a ton of shops."

"I'm sure I can find what I need at the thrift shop. I hate spending money on new clothes."

Micah shakes his head, grinning.

"What?" I ask.

"I thought girls love to shop for new clothes."

"I don't. Everything costs ten times more new, and the minute you buy it, it's used. I might as well find quality used clothes in good condition and save myself the depreciation."

"I can't argue with that." He carries his empty mug to the sink.

I'm about to do the same when my phone chimes with a new text. Then another one. Both from Ricky.

**Ricky: where the fuck r u?**

**Ricky: u need to come home**

**Ricky: Robyn your scarring me. Call me back or at least txt me**

I'm thinking if Ricky was tracking my car, he'd know where I am, and he wouldn't be asking. That means he's not the one who's doing the tracking. Verne is. Ricky might not even know about the tracking device.

"I don't think Ricky put the tracking device on my car." I hold up my phone to Micah, and he comes near to read the screen.

"It doesn't appear that your friend is the mastermind." Micah frowns. "And that's actually bad news. I'm not too worried about your roommate. It's the dealer I'm concerned about."

Micah runs his fingers through his hair, smoothing out any tangles, and begins braiding. I watch him, amazed by how quickly and effortlessly he threads the strands.

I run back into the bathroom to brush my teeth and put my hair back in a ponytail.

Just before we step outside, I pull on my jean jacket.

"You need a proper winter coat," Micah says. "And boots, a hat, scarf, and gloves. We could get snow any day."

"Thrift shop," I remind him. "Maybe after I get off work today?"

He nods. "It's a date. Well, you know what I mean."

When we step outside, the chilly air hits me hard, stealing my breath. We hustle across the yard to the shop and enter through the back door. Once we're inside, Micah turns off the security system. "The code is 1208. It's my sister's birthday." He shows me how to arm and disarm the system.

The office is dark, as we're the first ones in. Micah switches on lights before he heads to the kitchen to put on the coffee maker for the others.

It's six-forty-five, almost time for me to leave for work, when Margie pulls up and parks in front of the office.

She rushes inside. "Brr! It's cold this morning." She smiles at me. "Good morning, Robyn. Where's your coat?"

"I didn't bring one."

"Well, you're going to need something warmer than what you've got on."

"Don't worry," Micah says. "I'm taking her clothes shopping today after she gets off work."

While Margie's seeing to the coffee, Micah and I head out. When we arrive at the diner, he gets out of the truck with me.

"I don't need hand holding," I tell him.

He opens the diner's door for me. "I thought I'd grab breakfast since I'm here." He takes an available stool at the counter while I head down the hallway to the employee lounge to change.

Cara's already in the women's changing room. She has her *Jenny's Diner* T-shirt on and is in the process of tying on her apron.

"Good morning," I say as I open my locker.

She frowns. "You're the girl with the bad transmission. My boyfriend told me all about you."

"Your boyfriend?"

"Tony. He works at Jackson's Auto Repair."

"Oh, right. Yes, that would be me." Self-consciously, I hang up my jacket in my locker and change into a Jenny's Diner T-shirt.

"Tony says you're gonna be around a while."

I nod. "Looks like it. I need to earn enough to pay for a new transmission. And now tires, too."

"Where are you staying? At the motel?"

I hesitate. "Micah offered to let me stay at his place."

Her eyebrows shoot up. "You're living with Micah? Wow. That's fast work."

I tie on my apron. "It's not like that. He's just being nice."

She scoffs. "Sure, he is." As she walks out of the changing room, I hear her mutter, "It must be nice."

I slam my locker door harder than necessary. I thought I'd left the whole mean girls thing behind when I graduated from high school. Apparently not. She doesn't even know me, and she's already coming to conclusions about me. Judging me. It's just like high school all over again.

I take a deep breath, stop to get a drink of water from the water fountain in the hallway, and head to the dining room. The doors have just opened, and there are only a handful of customers in the diner so far. I can hear Jenny in the kitchen talking to the cook. Cara is waiting on an old guy seated at the far end of the counter.

I walk up to Micah, who's seated at the counter, reading a local newspaper. "Has anyone waited on you yet?"

He puts the paper down. "Nope. I'm all yours."

When Cara and the old guy burst into laughter, I glance their way to find them both looking in our direction.

"Something wrong?" Micah asks.

"No." I turn to face him. "What can I get you?"

"The special, eggs scrambled, with links and toast. And coffee, of course."

"Coming right up." I grab a pot of fresh coffee and a mug and pour him a cup. "Your food will be right out."

He takes a sip of his coffee. "Thanks."

When I head to the window to turn in Micah's breakfast order, Cara beats me there, stepping in front of me, nearly knocking me off balance. "Breakfast special, Charlie," she calls to the cook. "Eggs over easy, with patties and pancakes."

When she's done, she takes a step back, her bootheel digging into my toes. "Oops, sorry. I didn't see you there."

I put in Micah's order and say good morning to Jenny and the cook—Steve. While Micah's food is being prepared, I go wait on some other customers who've just walked in. When the sheriff comes in, Jenny comes out of the kitchen to greet him and take his order.

A few more folks come in, many of whom I recognize from yesterday. They must have a lot of regulars.

After Micah finishes eating, he leaves cash on the counter and walks over to me. "I'll pick you up at three, and we'll hit the thrift shop. Do me a favor, Robyn. Don't leave the diner without me. Not for any reason, okay? Just to be safe."

I nod. "Got it. Thanks for the ride. I'll see you this afternoon."

I pick up his check and find he left a twenty dollar bill. His meal was only eight, so that means he left me a hefty tip.

As Cara passes behind me, she eyes the money in my hands. "I see you got yourself a sugar daddy."

*Sugar daddy!* Heat erupts in my chest as I turn to face her. "What is your problem? You know absolutely nothing about me."

She gives me a smirk. "I know enough. You roll into town, and all of a sudden men are throwing themselves at you."

"That's bull. No one's throwing himself at me."

"Well, Micah's throwing money at you. First the tow, then a new transmission, and now a brand new set of tires. And now I find out you're living with him. Like I said, *fast work*." She turns and walks away.

Jenny comes up behind me and lays her hand on my

shoulder. "Don't let Cara get to you. She's just jealous. Probably every young woman in this town has had her sights set on Micah at one time or another. Cara used to flirt outrageously with him whenever he came into the diner. It got so bad he stopped coming for a while. Things didn't settle down until she got with Tony."

Cara's comment eats at me all day, and she goes out of her way to make things hard for me, getting in my way, *accidentally* taking one of my customer's orders and giving it to one of her customers, making me look bad in the process.

When my shift ends, I head to the employee lounge and change back into my clothes. I'm still angry about the things Cara said. She doesn't even know me, so why is she being such a bitch?

I meet Micah at the front door, walk right past him and push through the door out onto the sidewalk.

He follows me out. "Something wrong?"

"It's nothing."

He's right behind me. "You're not acting like it's nothing. Did something happen at the diner?"

"No." Micah's done enough for me. I'm not going to involve him in my petty squabbles. I gesture to the grocery store next door. "Mind if I stop in there to pick up a few things? You know, *personal* things."

He gestures to the door. "After you."

I'm still grinding my teeth as I walk into the grocery store. *Sugar daddy, my ass.*

Micah follows me into the grocery store.

"Micah, hi!" says the woman standing behind the sales counter. She's probably in her early forties, with long curly brown hair pulled back in a loose ponytail. I do a double-take when I realize she's holding a baby girl on her hip.

"Come on, I'll introduce you," Micah says as he heads for the counter, motioning for me to follow. "Maggie, this is Robyn O'Neil. Robyn, this is Maggie Emerson—well, I guess it's Ramsey now. She and her brother, Paul, own the grocery store."

"Nice to meet you, Robyn," Maggie says as she shifts the baby from one hip to another. "I hear you're working at the diner now."

I nod. "Jenny was kind enough to hire me as a server. I need to pay for a new transmission."

Maggie winces. "Yikes. That sounds expensive. It's a lucky thing Jenny had an opening." She smiles at Micah.

"This is Maggie's daughter, Claire," Micah says. "I'm assuming if Claire's here, then Owen must be, too."

Maggie's eyes light up. "He is." To me, she says, "When I'm here at work, my husband stays home with the baby. But we had a big shipment of goods come in today, so he's here, along with one of my teenage sons, Riley, to unload the truck."

"You have a teenage son?" I ask. "And a baby?"

"Two of them, in fact. Claire here was a late-in-life bonus." She smiles as she leans in to kiss the baby's blonde head.

A man comes through the back door pushing a dolly loaded with boxes. He's a big guy with brown hair up in a topknot and a trim beard. He's wearing a muscle shirt, and his arms are covered with tattoos. A teenage boy follows behind him pushing yet another dolly laden with boxes.

"Claire's getting so big," Micah says as he reaches out to the baby. She grabs hold of his index finger and smiles, showing off brand-new baby teeth.

"I'll just grab a shopping cart and pick up a few things," I say.

As I walk away, I hear Maggie whisper to Micah, "I heard about your new friend. Tell me all about her."

I do my best to ignore them as Micah catches Maggie up to date. I pick up just a few things: tampons, shaving cream, razors, and soap that doesn't smell like a pine tree. While I'm at it, I grab some bananas and apples, and I splurge on a bag of sour cream and onion potato chips, as well as a six-pack of Coke bottles and a bag of mini chocolate bars.

Maggie rings up my purchases. "That'll be thirty-two dollars and eighty-three cents."

Micah automatically reaches for his wallet, as if he's going to pay, but I catch his eye and shake my head. I pull the day's tips from my pocket and count out the cash.

Micah grabs the grocery sack, leaving me to get the six-pack of Cokes.

"Thanks," I say to Maggie as we head for the door. "It was nice to meet you."

"See you around, guys!" Maggie says as we head for the door. "Micah, be sure to bring Robyn on Friday."

"What's Friday?" I ask as we set the groceries in the bed of the truck.

"A bunch of us get together at my sister's bar on Friday nights. The folks who work at the Lodge, Maggie and her husband, me, Ruth and Jack. And Jack's friends, if they're in town. We eat and drink, shoot pool, throw darts. It's nothing fancy. You're welcome to join us, of course."

I smile, thinking I'd love to see Micah in a social setting, letting his hair down, either figuratively or literally. "I'd like that."

We walk a block and a half to a thrift shop. It's small, but well organized and tidy. Micah follows me to the women's clothing department.

"I appreciate everything you've done for me, Micah," I say as I search through a rack of blue jeans. "I really am grateful. But you have to stop trying to pay for things. Like my groceries, for one thing. People are talking."

"Who's talking? And what are they saying?"

"Cara called you my sugar daddy today."

He starts laughing. "Seriously? She's one to talk. Tony spoils her rotten, buys her everything she wants. And she has very expensive tastes."

"Yeah, well, she implied that I'm using you. I have a job now, so I can pay my own way. I don't want to sound ungrateful, but when you pay for things for me, it gives people the wrong idea."

He sobers. "I'm just trying to help. But all right. I take your point."

I pull a pair of ripped jeans off the rack. "I'm going to try these on."

"Robyn, you might want to keep looking. I think those are broken." Then he winks at me.

"Ha ha. Funny."

I end up taking three pairs of jeans, four T-shirts, two sweatshirts, and two pairs of flannel pajamas with me to the changing room. Micah waits outside the door as I try things on.

"Throw what you don't want over the door," he says, "and I'll put it back."

"Thanks."

"What size shoe do you wear?"

"A women's eleven, or a men's ten."

He's quiet for a moment, and I realize he must have stepped away. He returns before long and hands me a pair of brown leather hiking boots underneath the door. "Try these on. They're practically new."

They're a pair of men's boots, but the size is right. I try them on, and they fit perfectly.

When I come out of the dressing room, Micah's holding a teal women's winter coat. It's one of those expensive brands that's rated for really cold weather. "How about this?" He nods to a shopping cart, where I see a pair of gloves, a knit hat, and a matching scarf.

"Wow. Now I have a personal shopper. That's not going to get people talking."

He grins. "I'm just trying to be helpful. There's snow

on the way. You need to be prepared."

I try the coat on. It fits. So do the other items. "They're perfect. Thank you."

I end up buying two pairs of jeans, three T-shirts, both sweatshirts, and the PJs. I take the boots, as well as the coat and accessories. The whole lot is just under fifty bucks.

Micah stands beside me as I check out, and he never once offers to pay for anything. We're making progress.

"Thank you," I tell him as we're leaving the shop.

"For what?" He takes the two bags I'm holding and carries them as we walk back to his truck.

"For restraining yourself. You didn't offer to pay for anything."

He tries not to smile. "It was touch and go for a while, but I managed."

I'm smiling as I climb up into the cab. The longer I know him, the more I like him. How is it this guy is still single?

## 9

### *Micah*

After we return to the shop, I walk Robyn to the cabin. I show her where the washer and dryer are and leave her to get started on her laundry. She's got a lot of new purchases to wash. "I'll work for another hour, and then after dinner I'll teach you about guns. We'll just start with the basics, like how to hold it and load it. How does that sound?"

She shrugs, looking less than thrilled.

"Don't worry. You'll do fine."

After instructing her to lock the door behind me, I leave the cabin and walk across the yard to the shop. After changing into coveralls, I head into the garage.

"Welcome back, chief." Pete is grinning at me. "It's nice of you to join us."

"I wasn't gone that long." I shoot him a scowl. "And don't call me that. It's disrespectful."

I have a painful history with my mother's people. And ironically, my maternal grandfather actually was a chief. And since he didn't have a son, I suppose I might have filled that role one day. But no. Life didn't work out that way.

When my Cheyenne mother met and married a white engineering student at University of Denver, her family disowned her. And by extension, they disowned me and my sister. We know next to nothing about my mom's family. When my mom passed, I was just a baby. Because our dad travelled so much for work, Ruth and I came here to Bryce to live with our paternal *white* grandparents.

"So, where were you?" Pete asks.

"After I picked Robyn up from the diner, we ran some errands."

Tony whistles. "Are you her personal chauffeur now?"

"Until her car is fixed, yes."

"I didn't know Jenny was hiring," Tony says. "It was news to Cara, too."

Tony's girlfriend, Cara, is one of the servers at the diner. It's a small world. Sometimes, too small.

I shrug. "I guess an opening came up suddenly."

This is getting worse by the second. If they find out Jenny hired Robyn as a personal favor to me—and that I'm the one who's footing the bill—I'll never hear the end of it. And I certainly don't want Robyn finding out. She's already made it clear she doesn't want me paying for things.

I grab a set of Mitsubishi keys off the assignment board. "Hey, if you guys don't mind, I'd like to get some work done." I head out to the lot to bring the car in for a simple tune-up.

"So, how's your new girlfriend working out?" Pete asks.

I give him a look. "She's not my girlfriend."

"Well, she's livin' with you, and you're chauffeuring her around. Sounds kinda cozy, if you ask me, just the two of you sharing a one-room cabin. If I remember correctly, there's just the one bed." He wiggles his eyebrows at me.

"First of all, no one asked you. And anyway, I'm sleeping on the sofa."

Laughing, Tony throws a shop rag at my head. "What the hell happened to your sense of humor, man? He's just ribbin' you."

The guys leave a little after five. Margie's already gone for the day, and the office lights are off. I finish up working on the Mitsubishi and head into the office.

As I lock up, I peer out the front window just as a black SUV with heavily-tinted windows drives slowly past the shop. Robyn's car is parked out front, but covered with a heavy tarp so it's not in plain view. If someone is looking for her, I don't want to make it easy for them.

The SUV slowly drives off, and I wait around a few minutes to see if it returns. Sure enough, it makes another pass, just as slowly, as it heads in the other direction. Maybe I'm being paranoid, but after finding a tracking device attached to Robyn's car, this SUV seems awfully suspicious.

When I return to the cabin, I knock, giving Robyn a heads-up. "It's just me," I say as I unlock the door and come inside.

Robyn is on the sofa reading on her iPad.

"Are you still reading about the physicists?"

"Yes, and don't knock it. It's good."

I shake my head. "You have the most interesting taste in reading. How about we watch more of that *Bridgerton* show tonight, after our gun lesson? I'll even make us a big bowl of popcorn." I realize, as soon as I say it, it sounds awfully close to a date scenario.

But she doesn't seem to mind. "I'd love to."

I cook up some fresh salmon filets for dinner, along with some roasted broccoli and cauliflower.

After we finish dinner and are clearing the table, I ask her if she's ready for her first handgun lesson.

She joins me at the sink, and we make quick work of the dishes. "Do we really have to?"

"Yeah, I think we do. When I was closing up the shop tonight, I spotted a black SUV driving slowly past the lot—twice. The windows were heavily tinted, so I couldn't see who was driving, or even how many people were in the vehicle. Does that ring a bell?"

"No. Ricky drives an old white Chevy, and I have no idea what Verne drives." She dries a plate and places it in the cupboard. "You don't know for sure they were looking for me."

"No. But I do know I want you to be able to defend yourself if the need arises."

She takes a step closer, and our arms brush. To my

surprise, she doesn't move away.

When I glance down at her, she's looking up at me. "I guess it wouldn't hurt me to learn how to hold a gun. Maybe I can bluff my way out of trouble."

*Bluff? Good God.* I lean closer and lower my head to murmur quietly to her. "I'd rather you be able to shoot your way out."

## 10

### *Robyn*

After we finish the dishes, Micah disappears into his ginormous closet. When he's been in there a while, rattling around, my curiosity gets the best of me and I go see what he's up to.

I find him standing in front of a large metal cabinet, the doors wide open. "What are you doing?"

He glances back at me. "I'm deciding on a gun for you. You need something that's relatively small and easy to shoot, but also effective."

I walk into the room and stare at the contents of his arsenal. There are three long guns in different styles. For the life of me, I couldn't say what they are. One of them is black and looks very military. Another one is long with a wooden handle. That looks more like an old-fashioned hunting rifle. There are also half a dozen black handguns in various sizes.

He picks up a small one and weighs it in his hand. "I think this is your best bet. It's a nine millimeter, but the recoil isn't too bad."

Just looking at the gun in his hands gives me the heebie-jeebies. "Micah."

"Yeah?"

"I don't think this is a good idea."

"Why not?"

"I've never even touched a gun before. I don't think it's safe."

He looks thoughtful. "Okay. I hear you. How about a compromise? Will you let me teach you how to handle a gun? Flip the safety on and off and load the magazine? Let's start with the basics and see where we go from there."

I shrug. "I guess so." But I don't think he'll be happy with me just holding it. He wants to turn me into a modern-day Annie Oakley. "I'm not Annie Oakley, you know."

He chuckles. "How in the world do you know who Annie Oakley is?"

"I loved watching old westerns with my dad."

"For starters, no, I don't expect you to become Annie Oakley. But I also don't want you to be helpless when it comes to guns. Sometimes a gun is the only thing standing between you and something bad."

"When Ricky pointed a gun in my face, I froze."

"This is why I want you to get familiar with them. So you don't freeze. Let's just see how it goes, okay?"

"Fine. But will you promise, if I hate it, you won't ask me to do it again?"

He hesitates. "If you absolutely hate it, then okay. But, Robyn?"

"Yes?"

"I don't ever want you to be in a dangerous situation, but it would be foolish to assume it can't happen. I mean, right this minute, Verne could have a team sneaking up on this cabin. And if they come, they're going to be armed."

"If that's the case, and I'm here alone, I'm toast."

"But if you let them know you're armed—you could

just fire a warning shot—it'll slow them down a bit, long enough for you to call for help. They don't know you're not Annie Oakley."

"So, I'm back to bluffing."

He shrugs. "It's better than nothing."

"All right. One lesson."

Micah grabs a box of ammunition and the small black handgun he chose for me and closes the cabinet. "The combination for the gun cabinet is the same code I use for the security system in the shop—1208. Remember that."

Micah sits me down at the kitchen table and lays out the gun and the bullets. He starts by teaching me the name of the parts of the gun—muzzle, chamber, slide, frame, sight, magazine, safety.

Then he lays out ten bullets on the table. "The bullets go into the magazine," he says, showing me that it's currently empty. He uses his thumb to press one bullet into the magazine, then another. And then he hands the magazine to me. "You load the rest."

I feel like I'm all thumbs as I try to hold the magazine in my left hand and pick up a bullet with my right. I try to insert a bullet, but it doesn't go in easily.

"Put some muscle into it," he says. "Don't worry.

You're not going to break it."

I push harder, and the first bullet clicks in.

"Good. Now do the rest."

It's easier said than done. By the time I insert the last one, my fingers are sore. "That's harder than it looks."

Micah grins. "You'll get used to it."

"I hope not. You said I wouldn't have to do it again if I hate this."

He nods. "That's right, I did. But don't jump to conclusions prematurely. Give it a chance." He takes the magazine from me and shoves it into the handle of the gun. It snaps in with a nice clicking sound. "Note the safety is on," he says, pointing to the little safety lever on the side. "The gun will not fire if the safety is on."

"Got it."

He pops the magazine out and hands me both pieces. "Now you do it."

Rolling my eyes, I shove the magazine into the gun handle.

"The first two rules in handling a gun are critical," he says. "One, always keep the safety on unless you're ready to shoot something."

"Okay."

"And two, never point the gun at anyone you don't

want to shoot."

I chuckle nervously. "That's a good rule. What's number three? I'm assuming there's a third rule."

The corners of his lips twitch. "If you shoot, shoot to kill. Aim for your biggest target, which is generally the torso. If you shoot to maim—like aiming for a leg or an arm—you're probably going to end up dead. So, go for the torso. And fire more than once. Three shots would give you a better chance at eliminating a threat. Got it?"

I stare at him like he's nuts. If he thinks I could actually shoot someone, he's crazy.

"Robyn? Got it?"

"Sure, Micah. I got it." I don't, but hopefully this will shut him up on the subject.

"It's getting late," he says as he starts to collect all the gun paraphernalia. "How about next time we go outside and shoot some paper targets?"

He's not going to give up. I want to say no, and make him honor his promise to give up on the idea, but he looks so proud of himself, I don't have the heart. "All right, fine. If you insist."

"Great. Now, let's go watch your show. I'll make us some popcorn."

# 11

## Micah

I follow through on my promise to make popcorn while we watch Robyn's show. I bring a huge bowl full of the stuff to the sofa, along with two cold bottles of Coke, and plop down on the sofa beside her.

Since I haven't seen season one of *Bridgerton*, Robyn decides it would be best if we started over from the beginning, so I can get up to speed. She starts the first episode, and then she grabs a handful of popcorn and pops it into her mouth. "Mm. Butter and salt."

"Of course."

The show begins with all the pomp and pageantry of the Regency period—fancy dresses, top hats, and horse-drawn carriages. "Is this like a Jane Austen movie?"

Robyn smiles as she reaches for more popcorn. "Just watch."

A voiceover narrator starts speaking. "Isn't that Julie Andrews?"

"Shh." She elbows me lightly. "All will be explained."

Then we see the inside of a house with a lot of kids. "My God, how big is that house? I can't imagine what it costs to heat. Imagine the electric bill."

"Shh. I don't think they had electricity yet."

"I know, but if they did—"

Robyn turns to me, looking very put out as she presses the pause button on the remote. "I'm sorry, is this boring you?"

"No, not at all." I manage to keep a straight face, but it's hard because she looks adorable when she's annoyed. "Please resume."

The show continues, with lots of dressed-up characters arriving at a huge building. The narrator starts up again.

"I'm sure that's Julie Andrews!"

"Stop talking."

"Wait! The queen is Black? Since when?"

I receive another elbow in my side, but her lips are curving so she can't be that mad. "Please, Micah, just watch."

"So, *she* falls in love? Daphne?"

"Yes."

"With whom? With that guy?"

"No, just watch."

"Surely not with *him*? Give me a break."

"No! I said watch."

The show continues, and eventually we meet the hero. "With *that* guy?" I ask.

Robyn smiles. "Yes, that's the duke."

The show is good, no doubt, but I'm much more entertained by watching Robyn. By the time the first episode has ended, the popcorn bowl is empty, so I get up to make more.

When the opening credits for the next episode start to roll, she asks, "Do you want to keep watching?"

"Sure."

"Does this mean you like it?"

"Yeah. It's interesting."

The episode continues, and I'm too wrapped up in the

storyline to bother Robyn with more questions. Toward the end of the show, I notice her starting to lean in my direction. I glance at her in my peripheral vision and notice she's falling asleep. It *is* late, and she had a busy day. By the time the episode ends, her head is resting fully on my shoulder. She's out like a light, and I don't want to move a muscle.

I set the empty popcorn bowl on the end table and grab the remote so I can turn off the TV. I switch off the lamp on the end table and sit in the semi-darkness for a while. Robyn really should go to bed, but I hate waking her.

Eventually, I shift her so she's sitting upright, so I can stand. Then I lift her into my arms and carry her to the bed, lay her down, and cover her up.

Of course, she stirs, gazing up sleepily. "It's over?"

"Yes, for tonight."

She yawns. "Thanks for watching it with me. I'd forgotten how much I liked the first season." She forces herself to sit up. "I need to get ready for bed."

Just before she slips into the bathroom, she turns back and says, "Thanks for everything, Micah. For the popcorn. Even the gun lesson. I appreciate what you're trying to do for me, and honestly, it wasn't as bad as I expected."

"I'm glad to hear that. I'll turn you into Annie Oakley in no time." And when I wink at her, she smiles.

* * *

The next morning, after dropping Robyn off at the diner, I return to the shop to work. My productivity this week has been crap. I manage to keep myself focused on work for most of the day, pausing at noon to grab a quick bite to eat in my cabin. Around two, I head back to town, planning to stop in at the tavern to say hi to my sister before I pick up Robyn. The bar doesn't open until three, but I know Ruth and Jack will be there getting the place ready for business.

Jack is standing behind the bar drying beer mugs when I walk in the front door.

"Hey, Micah!" Jack calls. "What brings you in?"

"Just thought I'd stop in and say hi. I'm picking up Robyn in a few minutes."

Jack sets a mug on a shelf overhead. "Can I get you something to drink?"

"Just a Coke." I take a seat on one of the barstools.

Jack grabs a glass, fills it with ice, then pours my drink.

Ruth comes around the corner carrying a box of fresh limes. "What are you doing here?" she asks when she spots me.

"Gee, thanks. I'm glad to see you, too."

"He's here to pick up his girlfriend," Jack says, grabbing another mug to dry.

I sigh. "She's not my—"

Ruth sets the box of limes on the bar. "Speaking of Robyn, I find it interesting that Jenny just happened to have a server position open up right when Robyn needed a job."

"So?"

"So? Did you have anything to do with that?"

"What does it matter? Robyn needs a job. She's broke, and she wants to earn money to pay for her transmission."

"So Jenny's footing the bill? You know she can't afford to hire an extra server when she doesn't need one."

"Don't worry. Jenny and I worked it out. I'm covering the cost."

My sister frowns. "Micah, we're talking at least a couple thousand dollars here."

"Yes, and you're not going to say a word to anyone, all right?" I toss a glare at Jack, who's listening intently to our conversation. I point a finger in his direction. "That goes for you, too, pal."

Jack mimes zipping his mouth shut. "Not a word."

I stay a while longer to shoot the breeze with my sister and her boyfriend. When it's nearly three, I leave them to head next door.

"Bring Robyn tomorrow night," Ruth calls. "She's always welcome."

## 12

### *Robyn*

Thursday is a good day. Cara goes out of her way to avoid me, and no one tries to hit on me. Well, except for one old guy who's got to be in his nineties if he's a day. He's harmless as he sits at the counter drinking coffee and working his way through two slices of Jenny's homemade cherry pie.

Micah arrives right on time to pick me up. "How was work?" he asks as we head to his truck.

"Good."

"Your transmission should arrive tomorrow. I should be able to get to it over the weekend."

"Don't work the weekend on my account. It can wait until Monday."

"I don't mind, really. I imagine you're anxious to have your own transportation again."

We pull into the auto shop parking lot, and Micah parks the truck near the entrance to the office.

"Make yourself at home in the cabin," he says. "I have a couple more hours of work to do in the shop. When I'm done, I'll start on dinner."

"I feel guilty that you're doing all the cooking."

"I don't mind. We've got to eat, right?"

I walk on back to the cabin and let myself in. I'd like to offer to make dinner for him for a change, but there's not a lot I can make. Maybe I could learn.

My heart skips a beat when my phone rings. It has to be Ricky. No one else calls me. I glance at the screen, and sure enough, I'm right. I feel like having it out with him, once and for all, so I accept the call. "What do you want?"

"Robyn!" He sounds relieved. "I've been trying to reach you for days. Where are you?"

"You mean you don't know?"

"What do you mean? I have no idea where you are. Are

you somewhere safe?"

"Yes."

"When are you coming home?"

"I'm not."

"What? Don't be crazy. You have to come home."

"No, I don't. It's clear I can't trust you, Ricky."

He blows out a frustrated breath and suddenly lowers his voice to a whisper. "Robyn, you *have to* come home."

"Is there someone there with you?" When he doesn't answer me right away, I know he's not alone. "Who's there? Is it Verne?"

"No, not Verne, but a couple of his guys. I can't talk long."

I hear what sounds like the kitchen screen door close and then footsteps on the gravel path. It sounds like Ricky stepped outside. "Listen, Robyn, you have no idea how much trouble we're in."

"*We?*"

"Yes, *we*. You know a lot about Verne's business. You're a liability to him. If you don't come back and work with us—"

"I already told you no, Ricky. Nothing's changed." Then I remember the tracker. "Did you put a GPS device on my car?" There's dead silence over the line, which makes me think I managed to shock him. "Ricky? Did you?"

"Of course not." He exhales. "It was one of Verne's men. He put it on your car so he could track you to Seattle and back. It was for your own safety, in case something went wrong. But that means they know where you are, Robyn, and if you don't come back—" He sounds truly spooked.

My heart slams into my chest. "I have to go."

"No, wait! They're out searching for you right now. You—"

"Goodbye, Ricky. I really just wanted to say thank you for everything you did for me. I'll always be grateful. But it's time for us to go our separate ways." Before he has a chance to respond, I end the call and put my phone on *do not disturb*.

I need to warn Micah, so I grab my coat, race across the yard, and enter the shop through the back door. I find all three of the mechanics gathered in the front office. The lights are off, and it looks like Margie's gone for the day.

"Micah," I say breathlessly, "Ricky says they're coming."

He turns to face me, his expression grim. "They're already here."

"What?" As I follow the direction of his gaze, I notice a dark SUV parked on the side of the road across from the auto shop. That's when I notice a handgun is tucked into the back waistband of Micah's jeans. "What do we do?"

"I've already called Chris. He's on his way, with backup."

Not thirty seconds later, we hear multiple sirens in the distance. As the sounds grow louder—closer—the SUV makes a sharp U-turn in the middle of the road and speeds off north, away from town.

A minute later, two police vehicles pull into the parking lot, lights flashing, sirens still blaring. They're definitely making their presence known. Chris gets out of his vehicle and walks up to the building.

Micah opens the door for him. "Thanks for coming. They took off as soon as they heard the sirens."

Chris's gaze lands on me. "Robyn, are you okay?"

I nod, not trusting myself to speak. There's a painful knot in my throat, and I'm trying not to panic. These people are in danger because of me.

Micah takes one look at me, walks over, and pulls me into his arms. "Hey, it's okay. You're safe."

The reality of the situation hits me hard. Those people followed me all the way from Denver. I pull back. "This is all my fault. I never should have come here. You're all in danger because of me."

"We don't scare that easily, Robyn," Chris says.

"Yeah," Pete says. "We're not afraid of a bunch of two-bit drug dealers."

Chris says he'll write up a report so he has something on record. Other than the make and model of the SUV, he doesn't have any actionable information. There was no license plate. Nothing to follow up on or trace. "My deputies and I will patrol the area heavily. If they come back, we'll catch them."

Pete and Tony head out for the night, and I wait with Micah while he locks up the shop and sets the alarm. We exit from the back door and walk across the yard to the cabin. I find myself watching over my shoulder and jumping at every little sound.

Once we're inside, Micah turns the deadbolt. Somehow I don't think a deadbolt is going to keep drug dealers out for long.

"Have a seat and relax," he says as he makes a quick sweep of the cabin, checking the closet, the bathroom, and the pantry. He double checks all the doors and windows to make sure they're locked.

When he's done, he says, "How about we whip up

something quick for dinner, and then have that shooting lesson?"

"Do we have to?"

Grimly, he nods. "I'm afraid we do, now more than ever."

* * *

After Micah grabs my gun, a few human-shaped paper targets, and two pairs of earmuffs from the gun cabinet, we put on our coats and head out the back door. I follow him a few yards into the trees. Many of the leaves have changed color and fallen, creating a crunchy carpet beneath our feet.

He tacks one of the targets to a tree, piercing the sheet of paper on an existing nail. Apparently, he's done this before. He draws me back away from the target, fits a pair of earmuffs on me, and then puts a pair on himself. "Ready?"

"No." I'm only half kidding.

He laughs as he motions me closer. "Come here."

To my surprise, he positions me right in front of him so that I'm facing the target.

His arms come around me, drawing me back against

his chest. "Always use both hands when aiming. Use your dominant hand to hold the grip, and this index finger on the trigger." He manipulates my hands to illustrate. "Use your other hand to support your dominant hand." He places the gun in my right hand, then wraps my left hand around the handle, positioning my thumb just so. "Good, just like that."

He shows me how to use the sight. Then he loads the magazine and hands me the gun.

"Ready?" He grips my shoulders to hold me steady. "Take your time. Flip off the safety. Aim, and then slowly squeeze the trigger. Be ready for the kickback and the noise."

I do as he said, squeezing the trigger. The gun kicks violently in my hands, and my aim goes wide.

He squeezes my shoulders. "It's okay. Try again."

I fire a second shot and miss the paper target, hitting the tree instead and knocking off a chunk of bark. "I'm terrible at this."

"At least you hit the tree this time. That's an improvement."

"Ha ha." I try again. This time I manage to hit the very edge of the paper target.

"See? You're getting it. Keep going. Empty the

magazine."

I fire again, completely missing the target. The remaining shots are better, but not by much. "If this were a real firefight, I'd be toast."

He pats my shoulder and hands me ten more bullets. "Here. Reload."

"But you said one lesson."

"That doesn't mean just one magazine. Shooting requires practice. A lot of practice. Now reload."

I load the bullets and shove the magazine into the gun. I fire all ten, my aim marginally better this time.

"Hey, you're getting the hang of it," Micah says. He holds out ten more bullets.

"No," I say, stepping away from him. "My shoulders hurt."

He quickly inserts the bullets himself and slams the magazine into the grip. "Are we done for tonight?"

"I am. But I want to see you shoot."

Micah hangs a new target and returns to my side. Without pause, he raises the gun in a practiced two-hand grip and empties the magazine, firing in rapid succession. He absolutely shreds the target, right where the heart would be.

"Show-off," I say.

"After a tour in Afghanistan, I've been in more firefights than I can possibly count. If I wasn't a good shot, I wouldn't be standing here today." He reloads, flips on the safety, and tucks the gun into the back waistband of his jeans. "Come with me. There's something I want to show you."

We walk deeper into the woods, following a well-worn dirt path until Micah abruptly stops. "See this here?" He points to a tree with a branch that has been sawed off. "Here's where you get off the path and walk into the trees."

I follow him through the trees, stepping over fallen logs and skirting around thick shrubs. It's starting to get dark, which makes it even harder to see where we're going.

When I trip over a small log, he takes my hand and steadies me. "It's not far now."

A few minutes later, we come across a small wooden structure nestled amongst the trees. It's hardly bigger than a shed.

"My grandfather built this decades ago. He let me use it as a playhouse."

He walks right up to the shed and opens the door. "Go on in."

"It's dark in there." The shed has no windows, so it's pitch black inside.

"Use your phone's flashlight."

I switch on my light and peer inside. It's tiny, barely wide enough for the single cot holding a stained pillow and a threadbare blanket. "What is this place?"

He chuckles. "I guess you could call it the original man cave. My grandpa built this back in the 1930s, when he built the cabin—the one I live in now. This was before he and my grandmother moved into a larger home."

I glance around the interior of the shed, underneath the bed, and in the corners. Even though it's barebones and old, it's clean inside. I don't see any raccoon droppings or giant spider webs. "Why are you showing me this?"

"I wanted you to know this place exists." He closes the door, shutting us inside, turns the deadbolt, and then drops a heavy iron bar across the door. "If you're at the cabin and you're in trouble, consider this a safe place to hide. You can sneak out the back door and disappear into the woods. No one besides me knows about this place."

"So, it's a panic room of sorts."

"Yeah, you could say that."

* * *

There's a loud thud against one of the cabin walls, and I flinch.

"It's just the wind," Micah says. He looks at me, gauging my response.

"Sorry. I guess I'm a bit rattled tonight."

"Tomorrow I'll install a security system in the cabin. If you're here alone, I want you to feel safe. And if there are any issues, I'll get an alert on my phone." He pulls out his phone and starts tapping on the screen. A few moments later, he sets it aside. "Done. It'll be delivered tomorrow. I'll wire the doors and windows. If anyone comes in, you'll be alerted, and so will I."

"I hate for you to go to all that trouble just for me."

He reaches out to touch my cheek. "It's no problem. I want you to feel safe."

Our gazes lock, and neither of us seems in a hurry to look away. The longer he looks into my eyes, the faster my pulse races.

His thumb, warm and a bit calloused, brushes my cheek. "I don't suppose there's any way I could talk you into quitting the diner, staying here on the property until we get to the bottom of this."

I shake my head. "I can't quit. I need that money. I can't pay you for—"

His brow furrows. "I don't care about the money, Robyn."

"Well, I do."

He winces. "I know you do. But what I care about is your safety."

"I'll be careful. I won't leave the diner without you. Besides, I don't think anyone would dare come into a public place like that to cause trouble. There would be too many witnesses."

"Fine." He doesn't look happy. "Do you want to watch more of your show tonight?"

"Really? You'd be up for that?"

"Sure. I love watching fancy dressed-up folk dancing and flirting and conspiring with each other."

We watch another two episodes, although this evening it's a quieter affair than it was last night. Micah doesn't ask as many questions. I think he's preoccupied by what happened earlier today.

I'm hyper aware of the fact we're sitting together in the dark, side by side, on the sofa. The only light comes from the TV.

I'm so preoccupied by his proximity. It feels like gravity keeps drawing me toward him. I can feel the heat radiating from his body. I glance down at his left hand, which is resting on his thigh. I study his long fingers, his blunt nails. With the lights off, his skin tone looks even darker. At one point, he must be getting hot because he pushes his long sleeves up past his elbows, and I'm treated to a view of his muscular forearms.

And now *I'm* feeling warm because I'm staring at the sexy veins running the length of his arms.

By the end of the second episode, I'm struggling to keep my eyes open. "I think it's bedtime for me," I say as the ending credits roll. "I call dibs on the bathroom."

He chuckles. "I think we've established that fact."

I head for the bathroom to get ready for bed. When I emerge, I find Micah on his phone. "No, we didn't get a look at them. Just the SUV. They took off as soon as they heard the sirens." He's quiet a moment, as he's listening to someone. "I already tried to talk her into quitting the diner, but she refused."

Another pause.

Then, Micah says, "I'd really appreciate it. Chris and his deputies are going to patrol the diner and the auto shop. I'll give Jenny a heads-up so she can be on guard."

Another pause.

After a moment of silence, Micah signs off the call, saying, "Thanks, Jack. I owe you."

"It's all yours," I say, trying to sound chipper, as if I wasn't just eavesdropping on his conversation.

I climb into bed while Micah uses the bathroom to get himself ready for bed. When he's done, he comes out and turns off the light over the kitchen sink, casting the cabin in darkness. Only a little bit of moonlight filters through the curtains.

On his way to the sofa, Micah stops beside my bed. "Can I sit a moment?"

I scoot over a bit to make room for him. "Sure."

Micah reaches for my hand and squeezes it gently. He brushes the back of my hand, sending shivers up my arm. Somehow those tingles find their way down my torso, and a liquid heat settles low in my belly.

"We won't let anything happen to you. *I* won't."

He sits there unmoving, just staring down at me. I think for a moment he might kiss me, but then he releases my hand and stands. "Goodnight, Robyn. Sleep well."

"Goodnight." I listen to his footsteps as he walks away, then lies down on the sofa. "You, too."

## 13

### *Micah*

I wrap up work in the auto shop on Friday around six and head to the cabin. As I let myself in, I disarm the newly installed security system. It's a simple wireless system that is configured to alert me if it goes off. The sun is setting already, and the sky is overcast, so the cabin's pretty dark inside. At first, I don't see Robyn, and my heart skips a beat. It takes me a moment before I spot her lying on the sofa, covered with a throw blanket, her iPad resting beside her.

Quietly, I close the cabin door and walk over to the nightstand beside my bed where I lay my phone and keys and switch on the bedside lamp. When I glance back at the sofa, I realize she's asleep. She's had a rough week, so it's not surprising she's exhausted. I stand there a moment, just studying her. Her face is soft and relaxed, her cheeks flecked with freckles. Her long auburn hair cascades over her shoulders in waves. For a brief second, I wonder what her hair would feel like as it brushed across my bare chest.

*Shit.* I have no business thinking along those lines. For one thing, she's too young for me, and for another, she's in a vulnerable state right now.

I grab some clean clothes from my closet and head for the bathroom to wash up after working in the shop. If we're going to Ruth's tonight, I want to get a shower first.

By the time I come out of the bathroom, Robyn is sitting up on the sofa. She sets her iPad down and gathers her hair in one hand and lifts it off her neck.

"I hope I didn't wake you," I say as I button up my shirt. "I tried to be quiet."

"I was just resting my eyes." She pats the sofa cushion beside her. "You're right—it's very comfortable."

I nod. "I told you." My gaze veers to my king-size bed,

where she's slept all week, and my brain goes where I don't want it to. She belongs in the bed—not with me in it, of course—but I can't help picturing myself there with her. "Are you still interested in going to the tavern this evening? If you're too tired, we can skip it. My sister will understand."

She perks up instantly. "I'd love to go. I haven't been out in ages. Not just for fun." She tosses the blanket aside and stands on bare feet. Her sneakers and socks are lying on the floor in front of the sofa. "If you don't mind—" she nods toward the bathroom "—I'll just freshen up."

While she's in the bathroom, I finish getting ready and dab on a bit of cologne. Not much. But I figure it won't hurt. I comb my damp hair.

When Robyn comes out of the bathroom, her long hair is in a single braid down her back. She's wearing one of her new pairs of ripped jeans and one of her new tops, a light green T-shirt with a V-neck that dips down to reveal a bit of cleavage.

*Damn.*

The sight makes my pulse speed up. My heart's beating so hard I can actually feel it.

Suddenly, I'm not too keen on the idea of taking her to the tavern. I can just imagine all the local guys who'll be hitting on her, not to mention any tourists passing through. "You know, if you're tired, we could just stay here." I point to the big TV. "We could watch more *Bridgerton*, if you like. Or, you could read." I gesture to her iPad lying on the sofa.

She shakes her head. "No, let's go. I'd love a drink." She walks up behind me. "Want me to braid your hair?"

The idea of her hands on my hair makes my heart skip a beat. "Sure." Of course I'm perfectly capable of braiding my own hair. I've been doing it practically all my life.

"Have you always worn your hair long?" she asks as she runs her fingers through my hair to make sure there aren't any tangles.

As she tugs on the strands, a shiver streaks down my spine. "Uh, yeah. As long as I can remember." Right now I'm struggling to hold onto a coherent thought. "I started doing it as a kid because I saw other Native Americans wearing theirs long and in braids. It made me feel closer to my mom. She wore her hair in a braid."

"And your sister does, too."

I nod. "I guess it's a family tradition."

Her fingers are quick and nimble as she weaves the strands together. At the feel of her touch, all the nerves in my body are firing and part of me is responding in a very inconvenient way. For a moment, I close my eyes and let myself enjoy the sensations.

When she's done, she holds her palm out. "Hair tie?"

I pull a thin strip of leather from my front pocket and hand it to her. "Tie it off with this."

A moment later, she pats my back. "All done. Now, let's go."

After we put on our coats, I set the alarm, and we exit the cabin. The sun is already setting, and we're losing the light. I don't think I'm imagining it when Robyn walks so close to me that our arms brush. I suspect she's a bit nervous being outside, especially near dark.

When we reach the parking lot in front of the shop, I open the front passenger door, and she climbs up into the cab.

"Thanks," she says, uncharacteristically quiet as she buckles her seat belt.

As I walk around to the driver's door, I'm very much aware that this feels like a date. It's a Friday night, and we're going out, just like any couple. Only we're not a couple. We're not together, and she's not mine.

Whose bright idea was this?

*Oh, right. It was mine.*

\* \* \*

When we arrive in town, the street parking is full, so I pull around to the parking lot behind the tavern. When we walk inside, we're hit with the dull roar of voices barely audible over the music playing over the sound system. The place smells like fried food, burgers, and beer. It's only seven, and already the place is crowded. That's typical for a Friday night. Ruth's Tavern is the place to be in the evenings, at least for the locals.

It's definitely a full house tonight. The barstools are already taken, and many of the tables are as well. Both pool tables are seeing action, as are the dart boards. There are even folks out on the dance floor already doing a popular line dance.

"Robyn!" My sister steps out from behind the bar to greet us. Or, rather to greet Robyn. She ignores me. "I'm so glad you could make it." She gestures to the bar. "Can I get you something to drink?"

"I'd love a strawberry daiquiri," Robyn says.

"On it," Ruth says.

"Actually, we should probably eat something first," I say.

Robyn rolls her eyes at Ruth, who laughs. "My, aren't

you the responsible one, dear brother?"

I notice a large group getting up from one of the bigger tables. We'll need that once everyone's here. "I'll grab our table," I say, leaving Robyn with my sister.

Casey beats me to the table and starts clearing it off, stacking glasses in a plastic tub before he wipes down the tabletop. "Hey, Micah, who's the hottie?"

"Her name is *Robyn*, not *hottie*." It doesn't escape my notice that Casey and Robyn are about the same age.

"Isn't she the new server at Jenny's I been hearin' folks talk? Her car broke down, and now she's stranded here?"

*Christ!* She's worked there five days and already folks are talking about her. This is what happens when someone new moves into a small town. There's lots of interest and idle curiosity. Especially from the guys.

"She single?" he asks, still watching her.

"Don't even think about it, Casey. She's off limits." Just the idea of him wanting to ask her out makes me want to hit something.

Ruth and Robyn have moved up to the bar counter, and now they're chatting with Jack, who's standing behind the counter pouring drinks. He hands Robyn something pink, undoubtedly a strawberry daiquiri, and Robyn takes a sip and nods, smiling. Then Jack hands her a tall glass of beer, and Robyn heads my way.

Grinning, she hands me the beer. "This is from Jack. He said you should drink it and lighten up."

"Thanks." I take a sip. "We still need to eat. I'm hungry, and I imagine you are, too." I take a seat, and Robyn sits next to me.

She picks up one of the laminated menus lying on the table and starts perusing it. "This place is packed."

"It usually is, especially on the weekends. It's the only bar in town."

Before I know it, Jess steps up to our table and smiles at Robyn. Our server is petite and curvy, with short dark hair and dark eyes. "Hey, Robyn. I'm Jess. Welcome to Ruth's. I'm glad to finally get a chance to meet you. So, what can I get you guys to eat?"

"I'll have a burger and steak fries," Robyn says. "Hold the onions, please."

"And for you, handsome?" Jess winks at me.

"I'll have the same."

"Coming right up." Jess returns to the bar to hand in our food order.

"She sure seems friendly," Robyn says, her eyes following Jess.

"She's curious about you. I think everyone in this

room is."

"Me?" Robyn frowns. "They don't even know me."

"Sure. Because you're new. And because you're pretty. And, it's a small town. We get our excitement wherever we can."

Robyn laughs as if I'm joking, but I'm not. I mean every word of it, especially the *pretty* part.

I notice more than a few pairs of eyes on Robyn. Mostly men, of course, but there are a few curious women staring at her as well. I should have thought this through. Now I'm going to end up acting like her guard dog, running off strangers. I can't help it. I feel responsible for Robyn. Her car is sitting idle in *my* lot. She's going to be sharing *my* cabin for the foreseeable future. That definitely makes her my responsibility.

Before long, Chris walks in, clearly off duty. Instead of his khaki uniform and hat, he's wearing blue jeans and a teal Henley shirt. When he spots us, he heads right over. He smiles down at Robyn. "Hi, Robyn. It's good to see you again. How's it going at the diner?"

Robyn smiles, looking genuinely happy. "Good. Jenny's a great boss. I really lucked out getting that job."

Chris meets my gaze as he says, "That is lucky."

I can tell he knows I asked Jenny to hire Robyn. Of

course he does. Jenny would have told him. When Robyn's attention is elsewhere, I glare at Chris, motioning for him to keep his mouth shut about the job.

Chris takes the seat directly across from Robyn. "Who else is coming tonight?" he asks as he glances around the bar like he's looking for someone specific. I have my suspicions.

"The usual suspects," I say. "Are you looking for someone in particular?"

"No."

"Right," I say.

Jess stops by to take Chris's order.

Not long after, the others start to arrive—Hannah McIntyre and her boyfriend, Killian Devereaux; Maggie and her husband, Owen; Gabrielle Hunter and John Burke; Maya McKendrick; and Travis Hicks. Except for Maggie and Owen, the others all work at the McIntyre Wilderness Lodge. They also volunteer for McIntyre Search and Rescue, as do I.

While Jess takes everyone's orders, I make all the introductions. The women seem quite keen on meeting Robyn. Maya claims the empty seat on Robyn's other side. Now, that's a scary prospect. Maya's a bit of a wild card, and there's no telling what will come out of her mouth. She and Robyn seem to hit it off right off the bat.

When I spot Jenny walking in, I kick Chris under the table.

"What?" he asks.

"Look who just walked in." I nod in Jenny's direction.

After spotting her, Chris glares at me. "Don't."

"Don't *what?*"

I grin at his discomfort. Jenny, Chris, and I grew up together. The three of us met in third grade, where we became fast friends. We must have been maybe nine years old at the time. For years, we were the three amigos. We did everything together, and life was good. We were inseparable all through school. After we all graduated, Chris went off to college to study law enforcement, I joined the Army, and Jenny stayed here in town working at the diner, which she eventually inherited from her grandmother.

Eventually Chris returned to Bryce and started working as a deputy in the sheriff's office. It wasn't long after that, when the presiding sheriff passed away, he was elected to fill the role. I returned a few years later after my commitment to the Army ended.

I've suspected for a while now that Chris has a crush on Jenny. But she treats him like a brother. She treats both of us like brothers, which is fine with me. But I don't think it's fine with Chris.

"So, Jen," Chris says, "how's the new server working out?" He winks at Robyn.

"It's working out great," she says. "Robyn has a lot of restaurant experience, so it was easy for her to get up to speed."

Jess brings pitchers of beer to the table, along with a variety of appetizers. "Drinks and appetizers are on the house," she says. "Courtesy of Ruth."

My sister joins us for a little while to visit with the ladies—her posse, as they like to refer to themselves.

"Oh, crap," Robyn says under her breath.

I follow the direction of her gaze as she watches a group of guys walk in and head for one of the pool tables. Tommy Hoffman's leading the pack.

I notice the moment he spots Robyn. When he smiles at her, she looks away.

There's a lot of bad blood between me and Tommy, and I have a sinking feeling it's about to get a lot worse.

## 14

### *Robyn*

Jenny seems genuinely happy to see me. She even tells Chris I'm doing a great job.

Now everyone at the table is staring at me, and I feel self-conscious. "I'm just grateful for the opportunity."

"Well, I'm glad to have you," Jenny says. "And now, speaking of the diner, I'd better get back over there to help close up." She slides out of her seat. "I'll see you tomorrow morning?"

I nod. "You bet."

"I'll walk you out," Chris says to Jenny as he stands and follows her.

"So, Robyn," says the pretty Asian woman sitting next to me. "What do you think of our fair town so far?"

Micah introduced us all earlier, but there are so many new names and faces, I can't remember them all. She's maybe a few years older than I am, probably mid-twenties. She's trim and fit, wearing blue jeans and a sweatshirt featuring the silhouette of a rock climber with the text *I do it with ropes*. Her long black hair is pulled back in a ponytail. Her pretty dark eyes are lined with kohl.

"I'm Maya." She offers me her hand, and we shake. "So, what do you think?"

"It's small."

She smirks. "You can definitely say that."

"I've lived in Denver my whole life, so Bryce is quite an adjustment."

Maya nods. "I get it. I came here from L.A., which is huge by comparison."

"What brought you to Colorado?"

She shrugs. "The rocks. What else?" She says it like *duh*. "I'm a climber. I go where the big vertical rocks are."

That makes me smile. "Are you with the search and rescue team?"

She nods. "I am." She sips her beer. "And I teach rock climbing to tourists at the Lodge."

"The Lodge?"

"McIntyre Wilderness Excursions. It's a swanky lodge just outside town where bougie tourists come to engage in wilderness activities—you know, horseback riding, hiking, camping, rock climbing. It's like *The Hunger Games*, but without the crazy people, and no one dies. At least that's the goal. We teach them to do fun, outdoorsy stuff."

Maya points to a dark-haired guy at the other end of the table, another plaid shirt wearer. "That's Travis. He's a rock climber, too. Beside him is John Burke. He manages the stables. If you want to go on a trail ride, he's your guy. Try not to stare, though." She bumps my shoulder with hers.

I notice the man in question has burn scars covering much of the left side of his face.

"And beside him, the redhead—that's John's girlfriend, Gabrielle. She's relatively new here. She runs the restaurant at the Lodge. And the couple at the end of the table—Hannah and Killian—they're the bosses. They own the Lodge and run the S&R team."

"S&R?" I ask.

"Search and rescue. And of course you already know our pilot, Micah."

She winks at me, which makes me think she suspects I know him far better than I actually do.

"He's fixing my car."

Smirking, she nods. "Riiight."

"No, really. That's it. He's fixing my car." And, well, now he's letting me sleep in his bed, but I don't mention that part. People are already getting ideas about us.

Maya nods. "Got it."

But I don't think she has got it.

I chat mostly with Maya for the rest of the evening. Micah's pretending not to listen in on our conversation, but I suspect he is.

When Maya offers to give me rock climbing lessons, Micah leans over and whispers, "I don't think so," in my ear. He sure is being bossy tonight, trying to tell me what I can and can't do.

I lean close and whisper, "Newsflash. You're not the boss of me."

That earns me a grin that makes my belly flutter.

On their way out, Maggie and her husband stop to say goodbye to me. She says they've got to get going because their daughter, Claire, who's at home with her big brothers, is throwing a fit and refusing to go to bed.

"She's got some new teeth coming in, the poor thing," Maggie says, nodding as if I should understand what that means. "She's been cranky for days."

The appetizers are disappearing from the trays, and somehow, magically, the trays are refilled. The jukebox is playing a mix of music, from old school country to some current pop songs. And Killian is telling us a story about his first encounter with a real-life 'gator back in his hometown in Louisiana.

I finished my drink long ago and feel like getting another. "Excuse me," I say as I stand. "Be right back."

I walk up to the bar to order another drink.

Jack is standing behind the counter. "Hey, Robyn. What can I get you?"

"How about another strawberry daiquiri? Heavy on the strawberry, light on the alcohol."

"Coming right up." He grabs a fresh glass and starts gathering the ingredients. "Are you enjoying yourself this evening?"

I nod. "It's nice to meet more of Micah's friends."

Someone brushes up against me, and I smile, thinking it's Micah. But when I glance over, I see it's Tommy. I step aside, putting some space between us.

"Good evening, Robyn with a *y*," he says. "Not the bird," he adds. "I didn't forget."

I have to admit Tommy's a really good-looking guy. Tall, with thick blond hair that flops over his forehead and blue eyes. I'd put him in his late twenties, about the same age as Micah and Chris. I bet they all went to school together. Tommy's wearing a pair of dark blue jeans and a fancy white dress shirt with mother-of-pearl snaps and one of those string ties. I guess this is him dressed up.

"Hello, Tommy." I turn my attention back to Jack, who's nearly done mixing my drink.

When Jack hands me my glass, Tommy lays some cash on the counter. "Her drink's on me," he says with a smile.

"Somehow I doubt that," Jack murmurs, ignoring the money.

"No, thanks, Tommy." I slide the money back to him. "I'm running a tab." That's not actually true. I just don't want him buying me anything.

Tommy glances over at the big table where Micah and the others are sitting. "I spotted you earlier sitting with Micah Jackson. Are you two dating or something?"

"No," I say, perhaps a bit hastily. "We're friends. That's all."

"I'm glad to hear it," he says.

As a popular Adele song starts playing over the speakers, courtesy of the jukebox, eager couples surge onto the dance floor.

Tommy holds out his hand. "How about a dance?"

"No, thanks." I pick up my drink and, as I start to walk away, he snags my arm.

"Robyn, wait." He looks me directly in the eye. "I owe you an apology."

"No, you don't."

"I do. When we first met, at the diner, I said something I shouldn't have. I was a bit forward with you, and I regret that. I'd like to apologize."

"Apology accepted. Now if you'll excuse me—" I try to pull free, but he tightens his hold.

"Don't go. Dance with me. Just once, please."

Even though he's not looking our way, I get the feeling Jack is paying rapt attention. Just one word and he'd—

"Just one dance, Robyn. Let me show you I know how to be a gentleman."

I'm already thinking he's doing a poor job of it, but before I can even formulate a reply, he takes the drink from my hand and sets it on the bar. Then he tucks my arm in the crook of his and walks me out to the dance floor.

"You look gorgeous tonight," he says as he pulls me

close. His gaze skims my body, finally landing on my cleavage.

I'm trying to decide between kneeing him in the balls or wrapping my fingers around his neck.

"Cat got your tongue?" he asks, grinning at me.

"No. I'm just trying to decide what to make of you. You're pushy."

His grin widens as if he thinks that was a compliment. "When I see something I like, I go for it."

I frown. "I don't like pushy men."

He ignores that completely, and instead he reaches out to touch my hair. "Your hair is gorgeous, like a dark flame." He reaches up and brushes his thumb across my cheek. "*You're* gorgeous. I almost didn't bother coming tonight, but thank God I did."

His touch sends a shiver down my spine—not the good kind, but rather the creepy kind. I attempt to pull out of his embrace, but he tightens his grip. "Let me go, Tommy."

"Oh, come on. Don't run off, sugar. We're just gettin' to know each other."

Suddenly, I feel a presence behind me, a firm chest pressing against my back. A pair of hands settles on my shoulders, and I know who it is even before he speaks.

Relief that Micah is here with me is palpable, so much so that I sag against him.

"I'm cutting in," Micah says.

Tommy's expression tightens. "Get lost, Jackson. We're just getting started."

"Robyn?" Micah's lips hover above my right ear.

"No, we're not," I say. "We're done." I attempt to pull my hands free from Tommy's, but he doesn't take a hint.

"Let her go, Hoffman." Micah's using a tone of voice I've never heard before.

"That's enough," I snap, tired of Tommy's high-handedness. I yank my hands free and step back against Micah, who drops his hands to my hips and pulls me into him.

Tommy glares at me. "Fine! Enjoy slumming with the half-breed."

I flinch at the racial slur. "You son of a bitch!"

I raise my hand to slap him, but Micah catches my wrist and pulls it down to my side. "Don't bother, Robyn. He's not worth it."

Tommy walks away and heads for the exit.

When I turn to face Micah, I'm seething on his behalf. To my surprise, he seems completely unfazed by the insult.

"You're quite the mama bear," he says, as if that delights him.

"Why aren't you pissed?"

"At Tommy?" He scoffs. "What's the point? He's been tossing barbs at me since we were in middle school. He's a spoiled rich kid who's had everything handed to him on a silver platter. I couldn't care less what he thinks about me." Micah threads our fingers together. "At the risk of being soundly rejected, I'd like to ask you to dance."

As I gaze up into a pair of fathomless dark eyes, tingles race through me. Butterflies careen in my belly. All good vibes. His broad shoulders block out everything and everyone, until it's just the two of us standing here. "I'd love to dance with you."

His expression relaxes, as if he's relieved, or even a little bit surprised by my answer. He takes me into his arms, and we start to move. His hands guide mine, gracefully, fluidly.

"I'll bet you charmed all the girls in high school with your smooth moves."

He laughs. "Not so much."

I frown. "I find that hard to believe."

"Not too many girls in my high school were keen to dance with the *half-breed*."

"Are you serious?" I'm angry for him.

"It wasn't that big of a deal. And now, they're not too good to bring me their vehicles when they stop running."

"You should refuse them business."

"Nah. It's water under the bridge."

Micah turns me effortlessly, and I simply follow his lead.

I'm still dumbfounded and pissed that anyone would toss racial slurs at him, now or back then. "People are such idiots."

He chuckles. "People are people. Some are awesome, others are big disappointments."

The song ends, and another one begins—*Make You Feel My Love* sung by Adele. I've always loved this song, but her version is one of the best.

As soon as the vocals begin, the crowd around us fades away, and my vision narrows to the man holding me in his arms. His grip on my hands is strong, firm, and somehow still gentle.

What started as a dance—more like a dare—has quickly turned into something more. Something I can't explain. His gaze is locked on mine, his expression suddenly serious, and I can't look away.

He releases my hands and slips his arms around me, pulling me even closer to him. When my breasts press against his chest, it feels so right.

Whoever is programming the jukebox really loves Adele, because the next slow song is one of hers, too, *Easy on Me*. We effortlessly move from one song to the next without missing a step. Micah presses a hand to my back, and the weight of his touch seeps into me, stealing my breath as heat rushes through me. When he begins to run his hand up and down my back, my knees go weak, threatening to buckle on me.

In a move based on self-preservation, I take a step back, putting some much-needed space between us. I feel flustered, overwhelmed.

"Is everything okay?" he asks.

"Sure." I glance over at the bar, where Jack and Ruth are both watching us. "I should get my drink before it melts." I give Micah an apologetic smile before I bolt, practically running back to the counter.

My drink is right where I left it on the bar.

Jack picks it up and hands it to me. "I kept an eye on it for you."

I gulp the icy liquid, drinking so quickly I end up with a brain freeze. I set the empty glass on the bar. "Can I have water, please?" I've had enough alcohol tonight. I need water before I lose my head and do something foolish.

Ruth gives me a small smile, but she doesn't say anything as she hands me a cold bottle of spring water.

As I twist off the cap, I glance behind me and see Micah seated once more at our table. My heart is pounding.

*What the hell am I doing?*

When I return to our table and take my seat beside Micah, he stands and pulls his wallet out of his back pocket, opens it, and fishes out a few bills, which he lays on the table. "Time to call it a night, guys. I've got an early morning." He looks down at me expectantly. "Ready?"

Nodding, I stand and reach into my front pocket for some of my cash tips from earlier today. "I'll pay for my own food and drinks."

"That's okay," he says. "I've got it."

Ignoring him, I lay a twenty on top of the money he left.

On our way out, we stop at the bar to say goodnight to Jack. Ruth's no longer there. I wonder what she thought of me dancing with her brother.

We walk down the back hallway and stop at the last door on the right, which is partly open. I spot Ruth seated behind a desk in a room that must be her office.

"'Night, sis," Micah says as he pauses at her door.

"We're heading out."

When Ruth looks up, I'm struck all over again by how much they look alike.

"Goodnight, you two," she says. "It was a pleasure to see you again, Robyn. Glad you could stop by. You're welcome back anytime."

Once we're outside, Micah walks me to my door, unlocks it for me, and opens it.

"I like your sister," I say as I settle into the front passenger seat.

He smiles. "She likes you, too."

"How can you tell?"

"She invited you back, didn't she?" With a grin, he closes my door and walks around to the driver's side.

We drive back to the auto shop in silence. I don't know about Micah, but my mind is back on that dance floor. It felt good to be in his arms. Really good. Maybe too good.

I glance over at him, wondering what he's thinking, but his eyes are glued to the road.

# 15

## Micah

I'm sorry about what happened tonight with Tommy. He has a general lack of respect for personal spaces—especially where women are involved."

Robyn snorts a laugh. "That's an understatement."

When we arrive home, I drive around to the back of the building so I can park near the cabin.

"I can see why you don't like him," she says as I'm unlocking the cabin door.

We step inside, and while I reset the security system,

Robyn takes off her coat and hangs it on a hook by the door.

"He seems like an entitled prick," she says.

I laugh as I hang mine up beside hers. "That about sums it up. He slept his way through the entire cheerleading squad our sophomore year of high school."

"Oh, my God," she says, snorting in laughter. "I'm sorry. That's not funny. Please tell me you're exaggerating."

"I'm serious. His friends on the football team bet him he couldn't sleep with every single cheerleader on the squad that year. He won the bet."

"That's just gross."

"Yeah, considering two of the girls got pregnant as a result, and he refused to take responsibility."

Robyn shakes her head in disgust. "And to think I danced with him tonight." She shudders. "Ew."

She's standing just a foot from me, gazing up at me with those amazing blue eyes of hers—eyes I could lose myself in. She's smiling and seems more relaxed than I've seen her before. The way she's looking at me has my body temperature rising, my chest tightening. Not to mention other parts of me.

"What about you?" she asks.

"What about me?"

"How many of the cheerleaders did you get with?"

I laugh. "None. They wouldn't have touched me with a ten-foot pole."

"Why not?"

"Are you kidding? Go out with the half-breed? Never."

Robyn shakes her head. "The girls in your high school were idiots."

"How so?" The look in her eyes has my heart pounding.

"For not recognizing what a catch you are."

"I was nothing but a tall, scrawny kid back then. I've filled out since."

"I'm sorry they called you that." Her soft pink lips flatten. "Kids can be so cruel."

I find myself staring at those lips. Even when she's unhappy, her mouth is mesmerizing, the corners of her lips turned down so expressively. I want to kiss that mouth, badly. I want to bite that pouty bottom lip and suck it into my mouth.

She fiddles with her phone a moment, then sets it down on the arm of the sofa. Music starts playing. The same song we danced to at the tavern—*Make You Feel My Love* by Adele.

I freeze, the air suddenly trapped in my lungs.

Stepping closer, she holds out her hands. "Shall we resume our dance?"

I hesitate only a second before I pull her close. The feel of her in my arms is everything—soft and warm. *Hell yes, I'll dance with her. I'm pretty sure I'd do anything she asked.*

We move slowly, our bodies pressed together. I release one of her hands so I can run my palm up her back. She slips her free arm around me, pressing her hand to the base of my spine. Heat rises through me, lighting my body on fire.

This has to be a dream. Surely, she's not wanting the same thing I want. I couldn't be so lucky. Our movements slow as the song comes to an end, and I expect her to step away, but then the song starts over, and I realize she put it on a loop. It'll continue playing until one of us puts a stop to it. And I'll be damned if that will be me.

It's during the third go-round of the song when she raises her arms and slides her hands behind my neck. She gazes up at me, her eyes locked on mine, seeking, searching. There's a question there. Although I'm afraid I'm imagining it.

She surprises me by going up on her toes and pressing her lips to mine, lightly, gently. Definitely asking a question.

I drop my hands to her hips and clutch them tightly. I'm so afraid of misreading her. Of misunderstanding. Making a mistake. "Robyn."

"Hmm?" Her voice is soft, her lips gently curving. She slides her hands slowly down my chest to my abs, then around to grasp my ass and pull me tighter against her.

There's no way she doesn't notice my erection pressing into her belly. "Are you sure?" I ask.

So many guys have hit on her since she came to Bryce. Men at the diner, at the tavern. Tommy. And she didn't give any of them the time of day. So, why me?

She pulls back to meet my gaze. "I'm sure. If you want—"

"I do." I pull her closer, this time wrapping my arms around her so I can feel every inch of her supple body against mine. I slide my hands up her back, one stopping to cup the back of her neck, the other slipping into her hair.

Hunger surges inside me, driving me to taste and touch her. I lower my mouth to hers, aligning our lips, nudging hers open. She sucks in a shaky breath, and then she opens to me. Her tongue meets mine, and our breaths mingle. Her hands move restlessly up and down my back, as if she can't decide where she wants to touch me.

But when she grasps my shirt and pulls it free from my jeans, it's pretty clear what she wants. She tugs my shirt higher, but she's not tall enough to pull it over my head. I grip the hem and do it for her, pulling it up and off and tossing it aside.

Her gaze latches onto my bare chest, her hands skimming across my pecs as she looks her fill. "You have a beautiful body."

That makes me smile. "I think you stole my line."

Her gaze returns to mine. "How would you know? You've never seen me naked. At least I've seen you shirtless before."

She's right, of course. "I—" The words catch in my throat when she grasps the hem of her shirt and starts lifting it.

"I guess there's only way for you to know," she says.

I stare, utterly captivated as she raises her top, revealing more and more creamy skin. A pale blue bra lovingly cups her breasts. She tosses her T-shirt onto the bed, leaving her standing there wearing nothing from the waist up but her bra. Without hesitation, she reaches back, unsnaps that bit of fabric, and lets it fall away, leaving her chest beautifully bared.

*Good God.* I swallow hard. My hands ache to cup those

perfect, plump mounds with their luscious pink nipples, but this still feels surreal, so I don't dare.

"Well?" She presses her lips together, I suspect in an attempt not to grin with triumph.

"Now there's no doubt," I say.

She grabs my hands and brings them to her chest, giving me a flashing green light. My discipline snaps. I pull her close, so that our chests are pressed together, the mounds of her soft breasts cushioned against me. My skin is hot, on fire. Our mouths find each other again, our lips claiming and nudging. Our tongues meet, tasting and licking.

I'm so hard right now I'm in danger of embarrassing myself. I can't remember ever wanting someone this badly. When I feel her nimble fingers working the fastener of my jeans, I intercept them and take control. I scoop her into my arms and lay her on the bed, desperately needing to slow this down.

I take my time undressing her, starting with her boots, untying the laces and tugging them off, along with her socks. Her jeans are next, followed by her matching pale blue panties. Note to self: she likes matching underwear and bras.

I've got her naked now, stretched out on my bed. I pull

her closer to the edge of the bed and spread her legs wide. She gasps, but doesn't object. No, she fists the bedding and watches me with anticipation. I glance down, and the sight of her hits me like a physical blow. Her pussy is absolute perfection, the lips pink and plump, her folds glistening with arousal. She's clearly on board. If I had any doubt, it's gone now.

I meet her gaze, giving her a chance to change her mind, tell me no.

"You'd better have condoms," she says.

I nod to the nightstand. "Top drawer."

She reaches over, opens the drawer, and pulls out a strip of condom packets. "Extra-large, huh?" she says, reading the packaging. "I like your confidence." She tears one off and throws the rest back into the drawer. She drops the condom on the bed, beside us, like she's dropped a gauntlet.

Right now all I can think about is making her come, with my tongue, with my fingers, and again with me buried balls deep inside her. I feast on her, stroking and teasing, smiling when her hips start to buck against my tongue, when her muscles clench down on my finger. I find that ridged spot inside her and stroke it relentlessly.

Her hips rise up to meet my touch. Her breathing

picks up, hard and fast. The sounds she's making, urgent and frantic, only drive my own arousal higher.

"Micah!"

Hearing her cry my name makes me even more desperate to sink inside her. When I feel her thighs trembling, when her pussy tightens on my finger, and her clit starts throbbing, I know she's close. Her cries are raw and shameless as she comes undone. Gently, I keep her stimulated through her orgasm, wanting to prolong it. She's beautiful, her eyes closed tightly, biting her bottom lip as she squirms in my hold.

When her body finally relaxes, I surge up and kiss her, letting her taste herself on my lips. I want her to know how good she tastes, how much I want it. I grab the condom packet, rip it open with my teeth, and quickly sheath myself. I shift to kneel between her thighs and lean forward, resting my weight on one hand as I use the other to guide myself to her lush, heated opening.

There's resistance at first, but she's rocking her hips to meet me, still giving me a green light. Once the head of my cock is in, she gasps, then surges up to meet me, driving me in halfway. She cries out, but it doesn't sound like she's in pain. No, that's the sound of pleasure.

I pull out a bit, then slide back in, over and over as I

slowly work myself into her. Her hands are on my shoulders now, pulling me closer. Her eyes are locked on mine.

I'm almost all the way in when I notice the first hint of strain in her expression, and I wonder if I'm hurting her. "Am I—"

"Perfect?" she asks. "Yes."

"I was going to say *hurting you*."

"Only in the very best way. Don't you dare stop." And then she hooks her ankles around my lower back and pulls me into her.

I sink the rest of the way, balls deep, and the heat and pressure are mind-blowing. "Robyn." I lower my mouth to hers and drink in her breathy cries.

I slow my movements, trying to give her time to adjust, but she's not having that. She rocks against me, driving me deeper.

I start moving then, slowly, pulling out almost all the way before sliding back in. She closes her eyes as if savoring the feeling of me inside her, and God if that doesn't make me even harder, something I didn't think possible.

I rock into her, setting up a rhythm. She cups my face and pulls me down for a kiss. Our breaths are hot and a bit frantic as the tempo increases.

"Yes, yes, more," she cries. "God, yes."

I'm amazed I lasted as long as I did. My balls tighten as I come swift and hard, my heart pounding, my breaths ragged. She digs her nails into my back, and that only jacks me higher. When I'm spent, I slow my thrusts until I pull out, careful not to dislodge the condom.

I drop down beside her and pull her into my arms. She's limp in my arms, still trying to catch her breath. I lean in and kiss her forehead. "Be right back."

After a quick trip to the bathroom to dispose of the condom and wash up, I return to bed.

"My turn," she says, and she races off to the bathroom. A few moments later, she's back in my arms.

We adjust the bedding so that we're beneath the sheets. She pulls me close, into her arms. "Sleep with me," she says. "I want to feel your arms around me."

I reach over and switch off the lamp. Then I spoon myself at her back, one of my legs between hers. She pulls my arm around her waist and holds it tight.

Robyn falls asleep first, leaving me awake to relive what just happened over and over. I know it was real because I have the evidence—her warm, naked body—in my arms. But honestly, my mind is blown.

And now that I've had her, I don't ever want to let her go.

# 16

## *Robyn*

I wake with a start in a pitch-dark room. It must be before dawn still, as no light is filtering through the curtains. I can hear the wind battering the window panes and occasionally a tree branch brushes the side of the cabin. But as blustery as it is outside, I'm toasty warm here in Micah's bed. *With* Micah. He's pressed up against my back, one of his legs intertwined with mine.

*I'm spooning with Micah.*

From the moment I first saw him, I was attracted to

him, but I never dreamed we'd find ourselves together like this. Ever since losing my parents, it's been hard for me to get close to people, especially men. My foster father was a creep, and the other boys in the home were troublemakers. But I find it easy being with Micah. He's so selfless. He's kind and gentle, and he wears his heart on his sleeve.

I'm not sure which one of us was more surprised by what happened last night—me or him. But after that dance, after having Micah's hands on me, I realized I wanted more. I wanted *him*. All of him. Life's too short not to go for what you want. I've learned that the hard way.

The heat of his body radiates deliciously against my bare back. He shifts in his sleep, murmuring something I can't make out as he tightens his hold on me, his arm around my waist anchoring me to him. Even in sleep, he's a protector.

I close my eyes and let my mind drift. I can't remember a time when I felt so comfortable, so at ease, so safe. I don't have to worry about who might come through that door. If someone does, I know Micah will deal with it.

As I snuggle back against him, my eyelids grow heavy again, and I feel myself dozing off.

\* \* \*

The next time my eyes open, I see the first hint of sunrise filtering through the sheer curtains. My bladder is full, so I slip out of Micah's arms and disappear into the bathroom for a much-needed pee break. While I'm in here, I brush my teeth, then head back to bed. We don't have to get up for another half hour or so, so I slide back beneath the covers so I can snuggle with Micah.

He rolls on top of me with a heavy sigh, pretending he's still asleep.

"I know you're awake," I say, slipping my arms around him. "You're crushing me."

He wraps his arms around me, pulling me closer so my breasts are pressed against his chest. He nuzzles his nose against mine.

"I wish we could lie here all day," I murmur, loath to leave this bed. To leave him.

"We can, if you want. Just call off today. Jenny won't mind."

"I can't. I need the money. My transmission isn't going to pay for itself."

"There's no rush, is there? Are you in a hurry to be someplace else?"

"No." I press a kiss to his bare shoulder.

"Maybe you could be a few minutes late then."

"Maybe I could." I slip my hand between our bodies and wrap my fingers around his heated erection. I can feel him throbbing and lengthening in my grasp as I tighten my grip.

He groans as he reaches into the top nightstand drawer to grab a condom.

Last night was fast and frantic. This time it's slow. Slow touches, slow strokes, slow kisses. Every touch is intentional. Every gasp says it all.

Once he's inside me, he rolls us so I'm on top. As I sit astride him, his hands are free to skim up my torso and cup my breasts. As I rock on him, setting my own pace, chasing my own pleasure, he focuses on my breasts, gently teasing my nipples. He leans up to suckle one, and then the other, and as they tighten, I feel a corresponding pull between my legs.

"Beautiful," he says, his voice low and rough.

I angle my position so he's hitting my sweet spot, and it's not long before my muscles are tightening and my nerves are singing. I bite my lip, trying to be quiet as my orgasm hits me like a tidal wave.

Micah leans up to kiss me, locking our mouths together. "I want to hear you," he murmurs against my lips. "Please."

I allow myself to trust him because the pleasure is too intense to keep all to myself. I cry out, my voice high pitched and keening. The sound sends him over the edge, and suddenly he's thrusting up into me, all the way, chasing his own climax. And he lets me hear him, his voice low and guttural as he shouts his release.

I wish we could stay just like this all day, but we can't. I have to go to work. We end up showering together, both of us sliding soapy hands over each other's body. After we rinse off, Micah guides my head beneath the spray, wetting my hair, and then he squirts my shampoo into his hand and lathers me up. As he's rinsing my hair, I realize how long it's been since anyone has taken care of me like this—not since my mom was alive.

I return the favor and wash his hair, although my arms are aching by the time I'm done because I have to stretch so high to reach the top of his head.

When we're done, we take turns drying our hair. He lets me braid his hair. Finally, dried off and dressed, we head out together, holding hands as we walk to the truck.

Everything's different now. There's a sense of closeness between us that wasn't there before. An energy. An excitement.

And as we head into town, I realize I can't remember ever feeling this happy.

* * *

Not surprisingly, Saturday is busy at the diner. We have lots of regulars coming in, as well as tourists coming and going from Estes Park. Despite the crush, it's a good day. The tips are great, and we have several large parties. Large parties often translate to large tips. Not always, of course, but fortunately, today they do.

Tommy Hoffman comes in at lunch, but Jenny spots him first and seats him at one of her tables. He tries to catch my eye, waving me over, but I ignore him. All I can think about is how he and his friends called Micah *half-breed* in school and ostracized him. That pisses me off.

When I come out of the ladies room, he's there, waiting.

"Hey, Robyn. It was great seeing you last night at the tavern." When he reaches for my hand, I yank it away, out of his reach. "You're not really dating Micah Jackson, are you?" He scowls. "Please tell me you're not. He's so far beneath you."

*Are we dating?* We've never actually gone out on a date. I don't think last night at the tavern counts because that was just a friends thing, and he invited me along to meet everyone before we started getting close.

I'm tempted to say, *"Dating? No, not really. But we're definitely fucking."* I would love to say that just to see the look on his face. But before I can get the words out, Jenny comes to my rescue. "Robyn, can you take table five for me? Thanks."

"No problem," I say, eager to walk away from Tommy. Jenny remains in place, an immovable obstacle in Tommy's way, until I'm gone from his sight.

Ricky's been calling me on and off all day, and of course I let his calls go to voicemail. I've listened to a couple of them during my breaks. He's worried and frustrated, and at times angry because I won't take his calls.

Each time he calls, he leaves the same message.

**Ricky: You need to come home, Robyn. Verne is furious. He knows where you are. It's not safe.**

Yes, I'm in a bad situation, but he's the reason. He's the one who tried to rope me into working for his dealer.

At three o'clock sharp, I hear the door open, and I turn knowing I'll see Micah standing there. Sure enough, there he is, but this time, it's different. He's even looking at me differently. I wave at him and motion toward the employee lounge, indicating I need to change. He nods.

As I hurry off to change, I notice Jenny coming up to chat with him, the two of them laughing. I have a whole new appreciation for Jenny and her long-time friendship with Micah. She and Chris obviously didn't treat him differently, or use racial slurs, back when they were in school. They stuck by him. And obviously, they're still friends.

By the time I'm back from the break room, Micah's smile has morphed into a frown.

"What's wrong?" I ask as he holds the door open for me. I step out onto the sidewalk.

"Jenny told me about Tommy crowding you in the back hallway. What did he say to you?"

I'm not about to tell him *exactly* what Tommy said—that Micah was beneath me—just more of his racial bullshit. "He asked if you and I were dating."

Micah's eyes widen in surprise. "What did you say?"

I shrug nonchalantly. "I said yes."

He opens his mouth to speak, but nothing comes out. Instead, his lips curve into a smile. "Really?"

"Yes, really. Do you have a problem with that?"

He shakes his head. "No, ma'am. I do not." He steps

closer. "If we are, then I guess you'd be okay if I kissed you, right here, right now."

"I would." My cheeks heat up. Right here, in public. In view of the diner and all the customers and staff. I notice Jenny watching us through the front window.

He takes another step closer, cups my face, and leans in to kiss me. It's a long and languid kiss. It's the kind of kiss that occurs between two people who have seen each other naked. The kind of kiss that says, *I want to see you naked again, very soon.*

I glance through the window and see Jenny watching us, a huge smile on her face as she gives me a thumbs up.

\* \* \*

When we get back to the auto shop, Micah tells me he's going to work a little while longer on my transmission.

"Can I help?" I ask. I don't know a thing about working on cars, but I want to spend time with him.

"Sure," he says. "Make yourself comfortable."

I bring a stool over and sit so I can watch what he's doing.

I'll feel so much better when my car is fixed. I'll be able to drive myself to work and run errands on my own. But of course I have no plans to leave Bryce anytime soon. I have a lot of money to save up so I can pay Micah back for the transmission and the work he's doing. That's going to take time. And even then, I don't even want to think about leaving Micah. We haven't talked about what's next for us—what the future will bring—but I hope this isn't a short-term thing.

Inside, it's cool and noisy, and it smells like motor oil and grease. Tony's using some kind of power tool to remove tires from a small white car. Pete's working under the hood of a red convertible.

I watch Micah work, having no idea what he's doing. I find myself preoccupied by watching his arms and hands move, watching his muscles flex and bunch, and admiring the sexy veins on his arms. Arm porn, for sure.

"Wrench, please?" he asks, winking at me as he points to a large metal tool resting on a stand.

I hand him the wrench.

He opens his mouth to reply, but before he can get a word out, his phone rings. After pulling it from his back pocket and checking the caller ID, he holds up an index finger. "Sorry, just a sec. It's Killian. I need to get this." He takes a few steps away to accept the call, listens a moment, then says, "Roger that. I'll meet you at the airfield in twenty minutes."

Apparently, I'm not the only one he chauffeurs around.

Micah pockets his phone. "You remember Killian, from last night at the tavern? He's asked me to fly up to a camp and bring down a guest who broke his ankle and can't hike down. It's not exactly a rescue. It's more like glorified taxi service."

"Right now?" I ask.

"Yep." He lowers the hood on the car. "Looks like your transmission will have to wait until Monday." Then to Tony and Pete, he says, "Duty calls, guys. I'm flying a medevac mission." He turns to me. "Want to come with me?"

"Seriously?" I hop down off the stool. "I can come?"

"Sure. It's a non-emergency flight. You can ride along and do some sightseeing from the air. There's always room on the chopper for one more."

My heart jumps at the idea. I've never been in a helicopter before. I flew in a plane once with my parents when I was five, but I hardly remember the experience. "You bet I want to come."

# 17

## Robyn

Micah calls the airfield to give them a heads up that he's coming to take out the chopper. While he's doing that, I go into the office to use the restroom and grab some water bottles and protein bars to bring with us.

By the time I come back outside, Micah's already in his truck waiting for me. I climb into the cab, buckle my seat belt, and we're off, heading north, away from Bryce.

It's a 15-minute drive to the airfield, and as soon as we

pull in and park near the office, Killian Devereaux pulls up in a dark green Jeep and parks beside us.

Killian is tall and fit, all lean muscles, with dark brown hair and a trim beard. He's wearing hiking boots and blue jeans, along with a black sweatshirt underneath a well-worn brown leather jacket.

Killian offers his hand to me. "Robyn." He nods. "It's good to see you again." I detect just a hint of his accent.

"Likewise," I say as we shake hands.

Micah points toward the office door. "After I file my flight plan, I'll start on the preflight checklist. She's already prepped, so the check won't take long." He disappears into the office, leaving me with his friend.

"I'm glad you dressed warmly," the man says. "It's chilly where we're going."

"Are we going up very high?"

"Not terribly high. Right now we're at 7,500 feet above sea level. The camp is another 1,000 feet up. But you'll definitely notice a drop in the temperature."

While we're waiting for Micah, I grab our water bottles and protein bars from the truck.

Micah returns a few minutes later, and Killian and I follow him to the helicopter.

"This is your helicopter?" I ask Killian as we watch

Micah begin the flight precheck.

"It belongs to the search and rescue organization," he says. "It's not mine personally, although I am licensed to fly it. I got my pilot's license a year ago so I could act as a backup in case Micah isn't available. Micah does most of the heavy lifting around here. I'm just along to push a few buttons as needed." He laughs.

Micah catches the last of that. "Don't let him fool you, Robyn. Killian is just being modest. He could fly this thing blindfolded if he had to."

Killian laughs. "Let's hope *dat* never happens." Again, a bit of an accent comes through.

"Your accent," I say. "Do you mind if I ask what it is?"

"It's Cajun, sha," he says, this accent thickening. "I'm from *da* Louisiana bayou, born and raised."

I stare up at the massive gray metal chopper. "It's bigger than I expected it to be." I ignore the male chuckles coming from the front. "How much does something like this cost?"

"It's a refurbished Black Hawk," Killian says. "By the time we outfitted it to meet our needs, it cost us a cool ten million. Fortunately for us, Hannah's brother Shane is loaded. He bought it for us."

"How many does it seat?"

"It can hold a crew of four, plus up to four passengers. Or, as is more often the case, two gurneys. It's a pretty robust S&R chopper."

After he finishes his preflight check, Micah waves us over to the chopper. "All aboard," he says. "Let's get you geared up."

Micah offers me his hand and helps me climb up into the body of the helicopter. Inside, it's all metal and dials and equipment.

Micah climbs in behind me. "Have a seat here." He gestures to a rather uncomfortable looking metal seat.

After I sit, he buckles me into a four-point harness. Then he tugs on the shoulder straps until they're snug. He hands me a helmet that includes a microphone, helps me put it on, and then he puts on his own helmet.

"Can you hear me?" It's Micah's voice coming through the headset.

When I give him a thumb's up, he smiles.

"Good. Now, listen to me, Robyn. You stay seated at all times. Got it? Do not release your harness for any reason. And don't get out of your seat."

Grinning, I salute him. "Affirmative, captain."

He smiles back. "Technically, I'm a pilot, not a captain, but close enough."

After the doors are closed and secured, Micah settles himself into the front seat on the left, and Killian takes the front seat on the right.

I watch as Micah starts flipping switches. I can hear him talking to the control tower and to Killian. Occasionally, Killian flips a switch or two. And moments later, I hear the loud whirring of the blades above us. I also *feel* them. The chopper vibrates wildly.

"All ready, Robyn?" Micah asks as he glances back at me for confirmation.

I give him another thumbs up. "Ready as I'll ever be."

The chopper shakes as we slowly lift off the ground. When it rocks a bit back and forth, I let out a squeal and clutch my armrests tightly.

"It's okay," Micah says. "Just sit back and relax. Enjoy the ride."

"You have a lot of experience flying, right?" I ask him, suddenly wondering if this is such a good idea.

He chuckles. "A bit."

"He's being modest," Killian says. "He evacuated injured soldiers from war zones, from hot spots, often under live fire. He's one of the finest military pilots I've had the pleasure to know."

The ground quickly falls away as we rise steadily into

a clear blue sky. Eventually, we veer off to the left, heading toward some distant mountains.

I listen to the chatter between the two of them as Killian fills Micah in on the person we're transporting to the hospital. According to Killian, there's a group of hikers up at a camp at 8,500 feet. "One of their members had a nasty fall this morning and broke his ankle. Since he won't be able to hike down, we're going to give him a lift to the hospital. There's no vehicular access to this remote camp. Guests either hike down or, if that's not an option, they're transported by chopper."

While they're chatting about procedures, I watch the passing scenery out my side window. The trees start to thin out, deciduous trees replaced by more and more evergreens and scraggly brush. I see more and more rocky outcroppings and steep vertical rocks tipped with snow.

"See that rock formation there?" Killian asks over the headset as he points out his window.

I look out the right side of the chopper. "Yes."

"Maya has climbed that rock face twice now. You remember Maya from the tavern last night?"

"Yes." The pretty Asian girl who sat beside me. "That's amazing."

"It's definitely an advanced climb. But that's Maya for

you. She knows no fear."

When Micah glances back at me and says, "Please don't get any ideas, Robyn," I laugh.

"Ideas about what?" Killian asks.

"Last night, Maya offered to give Robyn climbing lessons."

"And you don't want her to?" Killian asks, sounding truly perplexed.

"I don't think my heart can take it," Micah answers over the headset.

Killian glances back at me and rolls his eyes. "I see."

We haven't been in the air very long, it seems, when we level out, and Micah flies us toward a large wooden structure off in the distance.

"Here's the camp," Killian says, pointing out his window.

Micah circles the area, then lowers us in the center of a large, flat, grassy field. When we finally come to a stop, Micah and Killian release their harnesses and hop out of the chopper. Micah opens the door nearest me and helps me out.

It's cold up here, the wind biting, stinging my face. I pull my coat closer and tug my hat down to cover my ears.

Micah grabs a black bag, while Killian removes a gurney from the helicopter and rolls it toward the building.

We're greeted by a woman with blonde hair who directs us inside the building. "I'm Carla Richardson, camp director."

"Killian Devereaux, McIntyre Search and Rescue," Killian says as he steps forward and shakes the woman's hand. "This is Micah Jackson, our pilot. And Robyn's along for the ride."

"Thanks for coming, all of you," the woman says. "The guest in need of transport is resting in my office. If you'll come with me, please."

We follow the woman to an office just inside the main entrance, where we find a middle-aged man lying on a sofa, his bare left ankle wrapped in a white bandage and propped up on a cushion. It's clear to see it's a pretty bad break. The ankle and foot don't look right. The skin above and below the bandages is mottled purple and red, and the ankle looks misshapen.

Micah sets his medical bag on the floor beside the sofa and opens it. While he takes the man's vitals, Killian examines the injured ankle.

"Compound fracture," he says quietly to Micah.

Micah pulls some items out of his medical bag and

proceeds to splint the man's ankle. Even though he's being careful, the man grunts and gasps in pain.

"We'll take him to the hospital in Estes Park," Killian tells the camp director. "They have an orthopedic surgery unit."

Carla nods. "I can't thank you enough, guys. I don't know what we'd have done without you."

Feeling useless, unable to help in any meaningful way, I follow Micah and the gurney to the exit. I run ahead and hold open the door so Micah can push the gurney outside. When he passes me, Micah reaches out to squeeze my shoulder. He doesn't say anything, but his touch speaks volumes. Killian and the blonde woman bring up the rear, discussing follow-up plans.

I step back out of the way as Killian and Micah load the gurney into the chopper and secure it in place with tie downs. Micah lifts me up, and I take my seat. He fastens my harness.

"I'm pretty sure I can do that myself," I say, grinning at him as he tugs on the straps.

"I'm pretty sure you can, too, but it's more fun for me if I do it." He places a helmet on my head and fastens the chin strap. "Okay?" he asks. "Not too tight?"

I nod. "It's fine."

He reaches out to touch my cheek, just a gentle caress. His gaze drops to my mouth, and then back up to my eyes. He leans in, slowly, not bothering to notice that Killian is watching us with great interest from his seat up front. Micah presses his lips to mine, giving me a quick kiss. And then he taps the top of my helmet and goes to his own seat.

"Well, that was interesting," Killian says over the comms.

Once he and Killian are settled in their seats, the rotors start turning. The engine roars to life and the vibrations start up all over again. *Here we go*, I think as the grassy field beneath us falls away.

We fly to the emergency medical facility in Estes Park, and Micah sets the chopper down on a helicopter pad outside the ER. Hospital staff come out a side door to meet us. After Micah and Killian unload the gurney, the hospital staff take the injured man inside.

"That's it," Micah says as we take off on the final leg of our journey. "Mission accomplished. Back to the airfield."

It's a short flight back. After we land, Micah helps me hop out, and then he and Killian secure the chopper.

We say goodbye to Killian, who takes off in his Jeep.

Micah and I head back to the auto shop. By the time we arrive, it's dark, and the shop is closed up for the night.

Micah drives around the building and parks in front of the cabin.

"Thanks for letting me come along," I say as we walk inside. "That was truly an amazing experience."

He takes his coat off and hangs it on the wall. "My pleasure. I'm glad you enjoyed it." Then he holds out his hand for my coat. I slip it off and hand it to him, and he hangs it up beside his own.

"Actually that was pretty impressive," I say.

Micah smiles. "I'm a man of many hidden talents."

It hits me that he had a whole other career before running the auto shop. He flew choppers like the one we were on this evening, into hot zones, risking his life to rescue injured soldiers.

He turns to me, about to say something, but the words die on his lips. Instead, his gaze locks onto mine, and we both stand there staring at each other.

Finally, Micah breaks the spell. "We missed dinner. You must be hungry."

We ate protein bars on the flight from the hospital to the airfield, but that was hardly enough to sustain us.

I nod, not trusting myself to speak, because right now

my heart is beating double-time, and there are butterflies careening in my belly. My belly might be empty, but I'm hungry for something other than food.

"I'll make us something quick," he offers as he heads for the kitchen. "How about grilled cheese sandwiches and chicken noodle soup? The soup is canned, but it's pretty good."

"I can actually help with that."

Dinner isn't anything fancy, but I'm able to help. While the soup is heating in a saucepan, I cook the grilled cheese sandwiches. Micah sets the table.

I could get used to this kind of domesticity.

Micah comes up behind me, grips my hips, and leans in to kiss the back of my head.

*Oh, yes. I could definitely get used to this.*

# 18

## *Micah*

After we finish our late-night dinner, Robyn helps me clear the table. I wash the dishes, and she dries them and puts them back in the cupboard. I learned a long time ago that living in a small place requires constant clean up and tidying, or else the place deteriorates quickly. I didn't ask Robyn to pitch in. She did it automatically. It's nice having someone to share the chores with.

Once the kitchen is cleaned up, Robyn disappears

into the bathroom, I assume to get ready for bed. She re-emerges with her hair freshly brushed and up in a messy bun, and she smells like peppermint toothpaste.

"Ready for bed?" I ask. I suspect she's tired. She's had a long week and more than her fair share of stress.

She climbs into bed with her mini iPad. "I'm tired, but I'm not sleepy, if that makes any sense. I think I'm still wired from the helicopter flight. Do you mind if I read a while?"

"Of course not," I say as I turn off all the lights and set the alarm system. "In fact, I'll join you."

I hit the john myself to get ready for bed. Then I grab the hardcover I'm currently reading and stretch out on the bed beside her.

"What's that?" she asks.

"It's a military special ops thriller. One of Hannah's brothers is an author. He's a former Navy SEAL, so he knows what he's talking about."

She peers over at my book. "Is it good?"

"Yes. What about you? What are you reading?"

She chuckles. "It's a romance novel. Ironically, it's about a Navy SEAL. So, basically, we're reading the same thing, only my characters have sex. Do yours?"

Now it's my turn to chuckle. "My guy is currently at

risk of bleeding out in the desert, so he's kinda too busy to think about sex."

"Makes sense," she says. "Maybe he'll get lucky later."

"For his sake, I hope you're right."

I catch her smiling at me. That is, until her phone rings. She picks it up, glances at the screen, and frowns as she silences the ringer. I think this is the third time I've seen her do that in the past two days.

She glances at me briefly, then looks back at her iPad.

"Who keeps calling you?" I ask.

She shrugs. "Ricky."

"You don't want to talk to him?"

"No. He's pressuring me to return to Denver."

"Oh, hell no. Then don't answer."

Her lips flatten, tightening, but she keeps her gaze on her tablet. "It's just hard for me to accept the fact he betrayed me this way. He knew I'd never want any part of drug dealing. He was the only friend I had growing up, and now—he's, well, there's no coming back from this."

"I'm sorry. But, Robyn?"

"Yeah?"

"You have friends now, people who care about you. People who will protect you. I'm at the top of that list."

She stills, swallowing hard, and I get the feeling she's

trying not to cry. She's tough, I'll give her that. She's strong. Fiercely independent. These are admirable traits. But still, if she's hurting, I want to be there for her.

Her blue eyes flash over at me, and for a split second I see uncertainty in their depths. I take in her face, her broad pale cheeks, the light dusting of cinnamon-colored freckles across the bridge of her nose. Her lips, wide and dusky pink, are currently pressed together. Her hair, such a deep, dark red with highlights of gold, contrasts starkly with the white pillowcase.

An image flashes in my mind of Robyn last night in bed, her hair down, as she sat astride me, rolling her hips as she chased her pleasure. I reach over to gently brush her cheek. "Robyn, I—"

"It's late, and I'm tired. I really don't want to talk about it." She closes her iPad case and sets in on the nightstand. "Can we just go to sleep?"

"Of course. Do you want me to sleep on the sofa?" Maybe I've pushed her too far.

"No." She grabs my arm. "Stay with me. Please." She rolls to face me and presses a kiss to my lips. "Thank you for asking, and thank you for caring."

I thread my fingers into her hair. "You don't need to thank me. But since you did, you're welcome."

# 19

## Robyn

We spend all day Sunday lazing around the cabin, relaxing, reading, and watching more *Bridgerton*. The sex scenes between Daphne and the duke give Micah ideas, and we end up making out on the sofa. We cook together, do a bit of laundry, and even take a hike in the woods. We make a pit stop at the old shed in the woods. He even talks me into another shooting lesson. This one goes much better than the first one, and I actually hit the target more often than I miss it.

My ears are ringing by the time we finish—even with protection. "God, I hope I don't ever need to use this thing."

"I hope so, too," Micah says. And then he proceeds to make me load the magazine again.

"This is harder than it looks. I swear, my fingers are going to fall off."

When I'm done, he kisses my fingertips, one at a time. "Let's hope that's not the case."

After lunch, Micah spends some time outside chopping wood. He's got a lean-to behind the cabin that's full of neatly stacked logs intended for the woodstove. I'm enjoying watching him do his lumberjack thing.

\* \* \*

On Monday morning, I wake with a groan. It's back to work today. I check the time and realize I'd better drag myself out of this warm and cozy bed and get ready or I'll be late. Micah's spot next to me is empty, and I hear water running in the shower. It looks like he beat me to it.

When I hear the blow dryer in the bathroom, I imagine him drying his hair. When he emerges from the bathroom, wearing blue jeans and nothing else, my jaw drops. I can't stop staring at his bare chest, at all that smooth, warm copper-brown skin. And those abs! The guy has a real six-pack.

I read all the time about six-pack abs in romance novels, but how many guys in real life actually have them? Micah does, and he must get them from doing physical labor. In all the time I've been here, he's never once mentioned going to a gym. Instead, he works on cars and chops wood.

His hair hangs loose down his back. I've never been a big fan of long hair on guys, but now I'm a convert. On him, it's devastating. I could melt from just looking at him.

I watch as he prepares his hair for braiding by smoothing the strands and securing them in a ponytail. And then, without even seeing what he's doing, he reaches back to separate the strands into three equal sections and quickly weaves them together. He secures the ends with another hair tie.

"How did you learn to do that? Mine always turns out a lopsided mess."

"Ruth taught me, and our mom taught her. Want me

to braid yours?"

"Seriously?"

"Sure. It'll just take a few seconds. We have time."

"It takes me forever, and I still do a bad job of it."

Micah steps closer and takes the comb from me. "Turn around."

I do as instructed, and a moment later I feel him dragging the comb through my hair. I'd already worked out the tangles, so it slides easily through the long strands. Delicious tingles race up and down my spine, and I can't stop myself from shivering. If he notices, he doesn't say anything.

After he's made sure my hair is tangle-free, he lays the comb on the kitchen table and runs his fingers through my hair, carefully dividing it into sections. His touch is firm and confident as he quickly braids the sections, tugging on my hair, which sends more tingles down my spine. He's done in less than a minute.

"Where's your hair tie?" he asks.

I raise my right hand, showing him the elastic tie wrapped around my wrist.

He pulls it off gently and secures the ends of my braid with a few wraps of the tie. "All done." He lays his hands on my shoulders and gives them a light squeeze, brushing his thumbs against the back of my neck. His voice drops when he says, "Look at the time. We should go."

"Right." I pull on clean socks and my sneakers, and then I gather my phone and purse. We pull on our coats, and then he opens the door for me. We step out into blustery cold wind.

There's a light dusting of snow on the ground, signaling that winter isn't far away.

* * *

When I arrive at the diner with two minutes to spare, I kick the snow off my boots and rush down the hall that leads to the employee lounge. I put my purse in my locker and change into my work T-shirt. Just as I'm tying on my apron, I hear a toilet flush in the adjacent women's restroom. The door to the bathroom opens and out walks one of the servers I haven't had a chance to meet yet. She tends to work the evenings, and she arrives about the time I'm leaving.

She stops in her tracks and stares at me. "You must be Robyn."

I grin. "Guilty as charged."

"I'm Michelle." Her voice is stiff. No smile. She just

stares at me.

She's about my height, five-foot-seven or so, with straight black hair that hangs in a bob just below her chin. Her eyes are a dark caramel color.

"Have you worked here long?" I ask, hoping to break the ice. If I didn't know better, I'd think she dislikes me, but that's impossible. We've never even met.

"Two years." Her eyes narrow on me, and suddenly the air is thick with tension. Then she frowns and shakes her head before turning and walking out of the lounge. She mutters something under her breath, but I can't make it out.

I finish tying my apron and close my locker. Then I wash my hands in the bathroom and head out into the dining room.

The door opens and an elderly couple comes in. They're here every morning for breakfast. I'm already recognizing the regulars. I grab two mugs and a coffee pot and walk over to their booth in front of the window to greet them.

Maggie from the grocery store next door comes through the connecting door to pick up some donuts for her store.

I see a few more familiar faces throughout the day.

Chris stops in for breakfast and sits at the counter to chat with Jenny. Apparently, she made a blueberry pie that morning just for him.

A little while after the lunch rush thins out, Micah's sister, Ruth, and her boyfriend stop in to say hi to Jenny. They sit at the counter, but when Jenny's called back to help out with something in the kitchen, she asks me to step in to wait on them.

"Hi, guys," I say as I hand them each a menu. "What can I get you?"

Ruth smiles. "How are you liking the new job, Robyn?"

"It's great. Everyone's really friendly."

"That's small-town life for you," Jack says. "Everybody's nice, but they're also all up in your business, which sometimes isn't so nice."

Laughing, Ruth elbows Jack. "We'll both have coffee and the lunch special."

Today, that means chicken and dumplings served over real mashed potatoes—there are no shortcuts in Jenny's kitchen.

"Coming right up," I say as I fill out their ticket and clip it to the rotating order holder on the counter behind me.

"I heard you flew with Micah and Killian on Saturday," Ruth says. "How was it?"

"It was amazing. The chopper was bigger than I expected. The poor guy we went up to fetch was in a lot of pain, but he was a good passenger."

I pour coffee in their mugs.

Jack reaches for his cup, takes a gulp and winces as it burns his tongue. "Ow!"

Ruth rolls her eyes at me. "He is such a baby."

"That was *hot*," Jack says.

"It's coffee," she reminds him. "It's supposed to be hot." Ruth picks her mug up and takes a sip.

"Not *that* hot," he mutters. "It's like drinking lava."

I smile at the two of them. They make such a cute couple. It's like they're two halves of the same coin.

"So," Ruth says. "How's your new transmission coming?"

"Fine, I think. Micah said he'd be done early this week."

"I'm sure you'll be glad to have your vehicle running again."

"Order up!" yells the cook. "Two specials."

I hand Ruth and Jack their plates. "Enjoy your lunches. Let me know if you need anything." And then I head out from behind the counter on my way to check on my tables.

As I'm rounding the counter, Michelle walks right into me, bumping me rather hard.

"Sorry, Michelle." I smile apologetically. "I didn't see you there."

She looks me in the eye but doesn't say a word. I wonder what her problem is as I step around her and continue on my way.

The day passes pretty uneventfully. The only other familiar face I see is the sheriff's when he stops back in for a late lunch. The guy practically lives here. I have to wonder, though, what the big draw is? The food, or the owner?

"Chris!" Jenny greets him with a smile and a wave.

The sheriff returns her wave and takes a seat at a small table for two. He takes off his hat and sets it on the empty seat across from him. He's obviously on duty, as he's dressed in his uniform. I wonder if he's married. I'm kinda guessing he's not based on the way his gaze follows Jenny around the diner.

"Hello, sheriff," I say as I stand beside his table. "What can I get you?"

"Robyn!" He smiles. "Good to see you again. And call me Chris, please. We don't stand on formality around here."

"Coffee?"

He nods. "Please."

I turn over the clean mug at his place setting and pour.

"So, how's it going?" he asks. "Are you enjoying working at the diner?"

"Absolutely. I've waited tables in bigger, more stressful venues. This is a cakewalk in comparison. And Jenny's a great boss."

Just as I say Jenny's name, we hear the sound of her laughter coming from behind the counter. The sheriff leans back in his chair so he can see past me. I glance back to see Jenny talking to Ruth and Jack. The sheriff relaxes.

My curiosity gets the best of me. "So, is there a Mrs. Sheriff?" I ask.

Chris straightens and shakes his head. "Nope. It's just me."

Jenny and Ruth burst into laughter, and the sheriff leans back in his chair again so he can see them. "I'll have a burger and fries," he says, his attention still on the counter.

Jenny heads over to the sheriff's table. "Hey, Chris."

"Jenny," he says with a nod.

"I'll go put the sheriff's order in," I say, nodding toward the kitchen.

"Chris," he reminds me. "My friends call me Chris."

I guess that means he counts me among his friends. As I head for the order window, I glance back one more time to see the sheriff and Jenny in conversation. She's going on about something, and he listens with rapt attention. And when she finally walks away, his gaze follows her until she disappears into the kitchen.

* * *

When three o'clock rolls around, I head back to the employee lounge to change. But first I need to pee, so I walk into the ladies restroom. Both of the stalls are occupied, so I stand just inside the door, leaning against the wall as I wait my turn.

"I bet you a hundred bucks he's fucking her." That's Michelle's voice, coming from one of the stalls.

"Of course he is," another woman says. Cara, I think. "How else did she get the job?"

"She just walks in the place and acts like she's entitled." Michelle again. "Everyone fawns over her. The sheriff, Jack, and of course Micah. He's the only reason Jenny hired her in the first place. To make Micah happy.

You know Jenny will do anything Micah asks."

"So much for overtime hours now," Cara says. "I was counting on the extra pay for Christmas, but then she walks in and ruins everything."

I stand frozen to the spot, listening to them and trying to piece together what they're saying. My heart is hammering now, my pulse throbbing in my neck. A flush of heat rises up my chest and into my face.

One toilet flushes, followed almost immediately by the other. And before I can slip out of the bathroom, one of the stall doors opens and out walks Michelle.

When she spots me, her expression turns to a scowl. "Do you get off eavesdropping on other people's conversations?" Her voice is sharp.

"What, Michelle?" Cara asks. The door to the second stall opens, and Cara walks out. When she sees me, her eyes widen, and she has the decency to look embarrassed. "Oh." She gives me a forced smile. "Hi, Robyn. I didn't hear you come in."

The sound of rushing blood fills my ears. I turn and walk out of the bathroom, open my locker, whip off my apron, and toss it into my locker. I don't even bother to change out of my diner T-shirt. I grab my coat and purse before slamming the locker door. I storm out of the break room and head for the front door. I spot Micah's truck as he pulls up.

When he spots me, he waves and smiles. At least until I push through the door and march right up to his window.

His smile drops as he rolls his window down. "What's wrong?"

"Is it true? Did Jenny hire me because you asked her to? As a *favor* to you?"

"Robyn—"

"Don't *Robyn* me, Micah. Answer the question. Did you, or did you not, ask Jenny to hire me?"

His expression tightens. "I did."

At least he's honest. Why doesn't that surprise me? "So, she didn't actually have an opening for a server?"

"She did not."

"Why did you do it?"

"Because you needed a job. I—"

"But Jenny hired an employee she didn't need. That's *costing* her money. *I'm* costing her money."

When Micah grimaces, my pulse goes up even higher. "What?"

He winces. "I'm reimbursing her."

"Wait—what? You're *paying* her to hire me? So, in effect, you're paying my salary?"

He shrugs. "I guess you could put it that way."

"Oh, my God! So, you're essentially giving me the money to repay you for the transmission. You're going to end up paying for the transmission yourself, out of your own pocket." I know the sound of my voice is escalating, but I can't help it. "I can't believe you did that behind my back! What part of *no charity* did you not understand?"

"Robyn—" His attention shifts to the sidewalk behind me.

I turn to see Ruth standing just a few feet away from us, hands on her hips. "What in the hell is going on out here? I could hear Robyn from inside the bar."

"It's complicated," Micah says.

"It's really not!" I turn to Ruth. "Your brother is a terrible business person."

Ruth's obviously trying not to smile. "Is that so?"

"Yes." I turn back to Micah. "Please tell Jenny I quit. It's not her fault—she's great—but I won't be a party to this."

"A party to what?" Ruth asks.

"Your brother asked Jenny to hire me as a server as a *favor* to him. The other servers hate me for it, and I don't blame them one bit. I'd hate me, too. And he's reimbursing her for the cost! That's why he's a terrible business person. He was secretly planning to foot the bill for my new transmission himself. That's nearly two grand, plus there's the cost of new tires on top of that!"

Ruth makes eye contact with her brother, and the two of them just look at each other. No expressions. Nothing to give away what they're thinking, and yet I'm pretty sure they understand each other.

"I'll hire you," Ruth says. "I actually have an opening. One of my servers gave notice today. The pay is minimum wage, plus tips. The job is yours if you want it. Monday through Friday, 3 to 11."

"I accept. When can I start?"

"Tomorrow."

I nod. "Thank you, Ruth." And then I turn to glare at Micah. "I can't believe you did this behind my back."

"Robyn, I'm sorry. I was just trying to help."

I turn away and start walking.

"Where are you going?" he asks.

"Home."

"Robyn, it's two miles," he says.

"I don't care. Maybe by then I'll cool off."

As I head for the road, he hollers after me. "Robyn, wait!"

I try my best to drown out the niggling voice in my head that says I'm being unfair to Micah. He was only trying to help me, and it was a very generous thing for him to do. But I'm too angry to back down now. I feel betrayed all over again. First by Ricky, and now by Micah.

I hardly make it a hundred yards down the road when I hear the engine of his pickup trailing behind me. I glance back to find him keeping pace with me. Even now, after I went off on him, he's still watching out for me. I feel like shit. I'm a terrible, ungrateful person, and I just want to cry.

## 20

### Micah

As I watch Robyn storm off on foot, I glance at my sister, who's now standing beside my car door. "Damn it, Ruth. How do I fix this? I thought I was doing a good thing, but obviously not."

"*You* thought it was a good thing. She clearly didn't."

I let out a heavy breath. "So, what do I do now?"

"Well, first of all, you apologize to Robyn for deceiving her."

"What? I didn't deceive her. I would never—"

"Did you, or did you not, go behind her back by asking Jenny to hire her?"

"Well, yes."

"Robyn's right. You are a terrible businessman."

"I am not!" Why do I suddenly feel like the little brother who's in an unwinnable argument with his big sister? "My auto repair shop is highly profitable, and you know it."

"But Robyn's right, and you know it. Now she has a job—a real job—where she's actually going to earn money so she can pay you for her transmission. Apologize to her, Micah. Tell her you meant well. She'll understand—once she calms down. Just give her some time."

I nod. "Of course I'll apologize." I put the truck in reverse. "Would you do me a favor and tell Jenny what's happened. Let her know Robyn won't be coming back."

Ruth nods. "I'll tell her. Where are you going?"

"To follow Robyn home, to make sure she gets back safely."

I drive slowly down the road back toward the auto shop, keeping my distance, but staying close enough to keep her in my sights. Knowing that she's been tracked here makes it far too risky for her to be walking anywhere alone. Plenty of cars and trucks pass me on the road, but I hang back. I can just spot her up ahead walking on the shoulder.

I see when she turns into my lot and disappears from sight. When I pull in, I find her waiting for me at the shop door.

I park and walk over to her. Her eyes are red from crying, and her cheeks are pink from the exertion of walking home in the cold.

I look her in the eye. "Robyn, I'm sorry. It was wrong of me to go behind your back and ask Jenny to hire you. I shouldn't have done that."

"I'm sorry, too," she says. "I shouldn't have jumped on you like that. I know you were only trying to help me. Still, you shouldn't have done it."

I refrain from smiling at her half-apology, half-not. "Please don't hold it against Jenny," I say. "She was only doing what I asked her to do."

"I don't blame her."

"So, do you accept my apology?"

She smiles reluctantly. "Yes. I know you meant well, but I don't want charity from you."

"Got it." On impulse, I add, "What do you want from me?"

"Just be upfront with me. No secrets."

"I will." I brush back her windblown hair, tucking some loose strands behind her ear. "I promise."

She draws in a swift breath and takes a step closer so that she's standing right in front of me. When the tip of her tongue slips out to wet her bottom lip, my brain misfires, and my heart starts pounding. "And, it wouldn't hurt if you kissed me," she says.

"You don't have to ask me twice." I kiss her then, relieved that she's no longer mad at me.

I reach out to cup the back of her head and pull her closer. She reaches up and cups my cheek.

We break apart when we hear a shrill whistle coming from inside the garage. I roll my eyes. "That's Tony."

She smiles. "I guess I'll go to the cabin, while you finish up work."

I'm tempted to go with her right now, but I need to make more progress on her car. "I'll see you later. How about tacos for dinner tonight? You like tacos, right?" *I'm not above bribing her with food.*

Her eyes narrow on me as if she suspects this is a trick question. "Yes."

"Good. I'll see you at six."

Pete and Tony are both busy with work when I walk into the garage bay in my coveralls and get back to working on Robyn's transmission. The radio's playing a 1970s music station. *Damn, they had good music in the 70s.*

I focus on the project at hand, going through the motions I've performed a hundred times as I listen to the music with half an ear, while my brain is fixated on the girl in my cabin. She's independent and strong-willed. She's proud and clearly offended by the idea of someone giving her charity. I know a lot of girls who like it when a guy takes the reins, but Robyn is different. Which means I need to be different.

Margie is just locking up the office for the day when she comes to the connecting door and pokes her head in. "Micah?"

There's something in the tone of her voice that makes me stop what I'm doing to give her my full attention. She looks unsure. Nervous even. "What is it, Margie?"

"You said to keep a look out for an SUV with darkly-tinted windows."

My heart skips a beat. "Yes? What about it?"

"There are two of them parked across the road right now."

*Two? Shit.* "Did you see anyone?"

"No."

I step into the office with Margie. Sure enough, there

are two black SUVs parked on the shoulder of the road across from my shop. "*Fuck.* Margie, lock all the doors. Turn off all the lights and close the blinds." I pop my head into the garage and yell, "Close the garage doors *now!*"

Pete looks up from whatever he's doing, takes one look at my face, and jumps to it. He rushes to the controls and pushes the buttons to lower the doors.

Tony glances over at me. "What's going on?"

"We've got trouble out front." I call Chris. "They're back. Two SUVs out front right now. We're locking everything down."

"Where's Robyn?" he asks.

"She's in the cabin." I need to warn her to stay put and turn on the security system.

"I'm on my way, with backup," he says.

"Thanks. Come in hot. The sirens might chase them off." I hang up and call Jack. "They're back. Two vehicles this time."

"*Fuck!* I'm coming. Where's Robyn?"

"In the cabin."

"Micah!" Margie's shout as she peers through a gap in the blinds turns my blood cold.

As soon as I reach her side, I gaze through the gap

she's using to see that the SUVs have moved closer. They're in my parking lot now. All their doors open and four men dressed in black, their faces covered with ski masks, stream out of the SUVs and take cover behind their vehicles.

Pete and Tony rush into the front office.

"Micah, what the fuck?" Tony asks as he peers outside. "What do we do now?"

"Tony, go get my Glock from the top desk drawer in my office. Bring the extra ammo, too."

Tony races off to do as I asked.

When he returns, I tell Margie, "I want you to go into my office and lock the door. Turn the lights off and stay away from the windows until one of us comes to get you."

Pete joins me at the window. "Did you call someone?"

"Yes. The sheriff and Jack."

"Micah, there's four of them and three of us. And we only have two guns."

"I know." I dial Robyn's phone. She answers on the first ring

"Hey!" she says. "Were your ears burning? I was just thinking about you."

"Robyn, they're here, and they're armed. Make sure

the alarm is set and get your gun. Make sure it's loaded."

She's silent for a moment. "Micah?" Her voice is shaking.

"Just do it, sweetheart. I've called for backup. Hang tight. Everything'll be all right. They don't know where you are."

When the shooting starts, I end the call. The perps open fire on the shop, shooting out the big plate glass windows in an attempt to intimidate us.

The driver of one of the vehicles signals to two others to break away from the vehicles and flank the building, one on each side. They're probably looking for another way in. But I realize as soon as they reach the back of the building, they'll see the cabin. It won't take much for them to realize Robyn might be in there.

I text Robyn.

**They're coming your way. Run and hide. You know where to go.**

Tony's at my side, holding my backup Glock. He sets a box of ammo on Margie's desk. "There was only one box."

"Yeah, I wasn't exactly planning on a siege."

We hear sirens approaching now, which means things are going to get even more interesting real fast.

More shots are fired from the SUVs, shattering what's left of the front windows, forcing us back to stay out of sight.

One of the perps rushes the front of the shop, heading for the front door. He's armed, giving me no choice other than to fire. I was hoping to avoid this, but I can't risk Margie and the guys getting hurt. I fire, hitting him square in the chest. He drops to the ground, writhing in pain as blood pools on the ground beneath him. I'm surprised he's not wearing bullet-proof armor. These guys are amateurs. Deadly amateurs.

"Shit," Tony says. "They're not fucking around."

"No, they're not."

A shot rings out, and Tony flies backward, hitting the ground hard. "Oh, man," he groans, clutching his shoulder as bright red blood seeps through his fingers. "Those fuckers shot me."

I drop to the floor beside him to examine the wound. "Pete, grab some towels, quick!"

Pete hands me a couple of hand towels. I fold them in half and press them to the wound. Tony cries out in pain.

"Pete, apply pressure to the wound."

Chris arrives on the scene, along with two more police cars. They park behind the SUVs, pinning them in. Now the remaining gunman is facing two fronts—the shop and the cops behind him.

My blood runs cold when I hear gunfire coming from *behind* the building. "Pete, keep pressure on Tony's wound until the medics get here. I'm going after Robyn."

# 21

## Robyn

When Micah calls to warn me that the drug dealers are back, I jump up from the sofa to make sure the alarm is set. Then I put on my shoes, just in case, and race to the closet to grab my gun and spare ammo.

When I hear the first gunshots, off in the distance, my heart jumps into my throat. I move to the front of the cabin and peer out the window just as two figures dressed in black slink around the side of the auto shop.

There are more shots coming from in front of the shop, and now it's a full-scale barrage.

*Oh, my God!* Micah is in there, and maybe Margie and Tony and Pete. I'll never forgive myself if something happens to them.

My phone chimes with a text message from Micah.

**Micah: They're coming your way. Run and hide. You know where to go.**

*Run and hide?* He means the shed out back. This is why he showed me that shack. He knew this could happen.

As the shots continue to ring out, I grab my coat and the big flashlight, and I race into the laundry room so I can leave through the back door. When I open the door, the alarm goes off, but I ignore it and take off running into the woods.

I don't have much time before they find a way inside the cabin. And when they do, it won't take them long to realize I'm not there.

Once I'm in the trees, I keep running, racing down the dirt path.

"Robyn!" It's a faint cry coming from behind me.

My heart thuds when I recognize the voice. It's not Micah who's calling for me. It's Ricky. He's here, too.

I keep running, getting farther away from the sound

of gunshots. It's starting to get dark, so I have to watch carefully to locate the spot where I have to veer off the path and go directly into the trees. It's more difficult going now as there's no clear path, and it's getting dark. I have no choice but to use the flashlight to avoid tripping over fallen logs. I hope I'm going the right way.

I hear voices behind me, coming closer. Ricky keeps calling my name.

Finally, I see the dark outline of the shed. I race inside and shut the door behind me, immediately turning the deadbolt and dropping the iron bar in place to secure the door.

After I scan the inside of the small structure to make sure I'm the only one in here, I sit on the cot. My hands shake as I lay my gun and the box of ammo beside me. I don't think extra ammo is going to do me any good. If I find myself needing it, I'm in way too much trouble to survive more than a few seconds. These walls are made of wood, so they're not going to be much protection against guns.

I put my phone on silent and lay it beside me so I can see if I get any more messages from Micah. I'm so tempted to ask him if he's okay, but I don't want to distract him.

"Robyn!" It's Ricky again, shouting from somewhere off in the distance. "It's me, Ricky! Where are you?"

I move into the back corner of the shed and crouch down low beside the metal bed frame. I try to remain calm because panicking won't help. As time passes, I hear Ricky's voice getting closer.

"Robyn!"

Suddenly, the door rattles as someone tests the lock.

"Robyn, it's okay!" Ricky says. He's standing right outside the door. "I'm here. No one's going to hurt you. Open the door. I promise you, we can work this out."

I remain seated, silent, my hands shaking violently. If I have to fire my gun, I'm going to miss. I'm not that good of a shot to begin with, but right now I'm so nervous I don't think I could hit the broad side of a barn if I tried.

The door rattles again.

"Robyn, please open the door." Ricky sounds scared.

And then I hear another man's voice, deeper and gruffer. "If she doesn't come out, I'm going in."

This time there's a pounding on the door. "You need to open the door, Robyn," Ricky says. "I promise I won't let them hurt you."

I glance down at my phone screen, desperate for a message from Micah—a sign that he's okay. A signal that he's coming. But there's nothing. I'm on my own out here.

I flip the safety off.

"All right, I gave you your chance," the gruff voice says. "Now step back."

"No!" Ricky cries. "Verne promised me you guys wouldn't hurt her."

There's a solid thud against the door, followed by another, and another, as if the two of them are scuffling.

The gruff voice responds. "Get away from the door, kid, or I'll shoot you first."

I hear more sounds of a physical struggle outside the door, and then a single gunshot. Someone cries out, and I'm pretty sure it's Ricky.

And then, silence.

A heavy fist pounds on the door. "Last chance, girl! Open the damn door. I won't ask again. We can do this easy or hard. It's up to you."

As I wait for the inevitable, I raise my gun and point it at the door.

Something heavy slams against the door, and the old wooden boards creak ominously. He does it again—I imagine he's throwing his shoulder into it—and some of the boards crack. The iron bar holds, thank God. Again and again, he slams into the door. The rusty hinges are starting to pull away from the door frame. It won't be long now before he gets in.

And then what? I don't know if I can do it. I don't know if I can actually bring myself to shoot someone. But if I don't, he might very well shoot me.

I don't think I'm getting out of this alive.

And then gunfire erupts outside the shed. It sounds like there's an army out there.

I'm still pointing my gun at the door, my hands shaking, my arm muscles aching.

As suddenly as it started, the gunfire stops. My ears are ringing.

"Robyn, sweetheart? It's Micah. It's okay." Someone tries to push the door open, but the iron bar still holds. "Honey, can you unbar the door for me? It's safe now."

I push myself up onto my feet. My legs are half numb and shaking as I stumble over to the door and lift the bar. The splintered door opens slowly.

"It's just me," Micah says as he pokes his head inside the shed. "I'm coming in." He steps inside and notices the gun in my hand. "Let me have that, sweetheart." He gently takes the gun from me, flips on the safety, and tucks it into his waistband.

I throw my arms around him, and he hugs me tightly to his chest.

Micah presses his lips to my temple. "Are you okay?" He releases me and steps back, holding me at arm's length. He uses a flashlight to inspect me from head to toe. "Are you hurt?"

"I'm okay. What about Ricky? I think he was shot."

"Yeah. He's alive, but it doesn't look good. Chris has called for an ambulance."

"Are you okay?" I ask. "What about the others? Was anyone hurt?"

"Tony took a bullet to the shoulder, but he'll be all right. And one of the deputies was grazed, but she's okay." He glances at my ammo and flashlight on the mattress. "You did good."

I laugh shakily. "Are you kidding? I was a terrified wreck the entire time. It's sheer luck I'm still alive. Actually, I owe my life to that iron bar. It held when he tried to break the door down."

Micah pulls me into his arms again, and this time he kisses me. I notice Chris standing at the door. I hear even more voices coming from outside.

When Micah leads me out of the shed, I see two bodies lying on the ground. Micah shines his light on Ricky, who's lying unconscious on the ground. Jack is using what looks like a jacket to apply pressure to his wounds. A few feet away from Ricky is a man dressed in black, wearing a ski mask. It's hard to tell since it's pretty dark in the woods, but I think I see multiple gunshot wounds to his chest.

"He's dead," Micah says. "There were four assailants in all. These two, plus two in front of the shop. Of those, one is dead and one was apprehended by the deputies. Chris notified the DEA, and they're sending a team here tonight."

"You okay, Robyn?" Chris asks as he scans me up and down. "You're not hurt?"

"I'm fine. Just shaken."

He nods, then steps forward to hug me. "Thank God."

Jack catches my gaze and nods. "I'm glad you're okay." And then he tells Micah, "Ruth's on her way."

We hear more sirens in the distance, most likely coming from the ambulance. Chris goes to meet them.

Micah crouches down beside Ricky and presses his fingers to his jugular. "His pulse is slow and thready, but he's alive."

"He's so pale," I say.

"He's lost a lot of blood."

Paramedics arrive on the scene with a gurney and begin to examine Ricky.

Micah collects my ammo and flashlight from the shed. He takes my hand and leads me back to the path. "Let's go home."

I feel numb as we make our way back to the cabin. People are coming and going along the path—cops and two paramedics. When we step out of the woods, we find Killian and Hannah hurrying around the cabin. They stop when they spot us.

"Everyone okay?" Killian asks Micah. "What's the status?"

"Tony and one of the deputies were shot," Micah says, "but their injuries are not life-threatening. Of the four perps, two are dead, one is injured, and one apprehended."

Hannah hugs me tightly. "Robyn, we were so worried."

The reality of what happened here tonight is starting to hit me, and I find myself tearing up.

"Let's take Robyn inside," Micah says. He takes my hand and leads me to the back door of the cabin.

We walk inside, and he sits me down on the sofa. Hannah joins me and puts her arm around me.

A few moments later, there's a knock on the cabin's

front door before Ruth walks in. She sweeps the cabin with her gaze, first checking on her brother before coming to join me and Hannah on the sofa.

Ruth takes my hand. "You're all right?"

I nod. "Thanks to Micah and Chris."

"Where's Jack?" she asks Micah.

"He's out back by the shed with Chris and the paramedics," Micah says. "Robyn's friend is wounded, but alive. The perp who went after Robyn is dead."

Ruth nods matter-of-factly. "Good." Then she releases a heavy breath. "Micah, the front windows of your shop are all busted out."

"Yeah, I know," he says. "I was there."

The cabin door opens, and Owen walks in, breathless. "I got here as fast as I could." He glances around the room as if taking attendance. He settles on Micah. "I'm sorry, man, but the front of your shop is torn up."

Micah nods. "So I've been told."

Jack and Chris show up next, coming through the back door of the cabin.

Ruth stands, and Jack walks over to give her a hug. "Before you can ask, yes, I'm fine."

"Ricky's on his way to the hospital in Estes Park," Chris says as he gives us an update. "Someone from the

Larimer County coroner's office is on the way to pick up the bodies."

"I'll go get some plywood and board up your shop windows," Killian offers. "That'll have to do until they can be replaced."

"I can help with that," Micah says.

"No, that's okay," Owen says as he claps Micah on the shoulder. "We've got you covered. You and Robyn stay here and relax."

Jack leaves with Owen and Killian to help with the temporary plywood repairs. Ruth and Hannah leave together.

After they're gone, the cabin suddenly seems overly quiet. I stand and wrap my arms around Micah. "I'm so sorry. You didn't ask for any of this. And now your business is damaged."

"Buildings can be fixed," he says, caressing my back. "People, not so easily. The important thing is that our friends are safe. Your friend, too. He's lucky he was already incapacitated when I got to the shed, or he would've had to deal with me."

"He's the reason I was in this mess to start with."

"I was trying not to mention that part. I'm not sure where you stand with him."

"Nowhere now. He betrayed me." I pull back so I can see Micah's face. "I want to know who shot the guy trying to break into the shed. Was it you?"

He nods. "I got there a couple of seconds before Chris. I made the shot, but Chris would have, too, if he'd gotten there first. Any of the guys would have."

"Are you okay with this?" I ask.

"Am I okay with shooting the asshole who wanted to hurt you? Yeah, I am. Pretty damn good, in fact."

When he tightens his arms around me, I realize he's shaking, too.

"I could use a drink," he says. "What do you say? Hot chocolate or whiskey?"

"I think tonight calls for whiskey."

## 22

### *Micah*

I pour each of us a shot of whiskey. As we're sitting on the sofa, sipping the liquor, I pull Robyn close.

She leans against me. "Is it over? Please tell me it is. I don't think my heart can take any more drama."

"I think so. Chris talked to someone at the DEA in Denver. They're going to arrest Verne tonight. They've got enough evidence to charge him with attempted murder."

When she's done, I take the shot glass from her and

set it on the end table. Then I pick her up and settle her on my lap. "Do you want to talk about what happened tonight?" I ask. I'm thinking maybe she needs to process aloud.

There are shadows in Robyn's eyes, and she's uncharacteristically quiet.

She sighs. "When I was in that shed, all I could think about was you. I heard the shots coming from the shop, and I had no idea what was happening, if you were safe or... not. Micah, if anything had happened to you—or to the others—it would have killed me."

There's so much raw emotion in her voice, it makes me wonder if she's feeling what I'm feeling. I realize we haven't known each other for very long, and yet I can't deny these feelings I have for her. How long do you have to know someone before you admit what you feel for them?

"When I heard gunshots out back, my heart just stopped," I admit. "All I could think about was getting to you." I link our fingers together and gaze down at our hands. When I think about how close she came to being hurt, I shudder.

"You might think I'm crazy for saying this," she begins. "I know we haven't known each other that long, but—

do you think sometimes you just know? Is it possible to meet someone and just click?"

"You mean like love at first sight?"

She laughs nervously. "You probably think it's nuts."

"Actually, I don't think it's crazy at all." When I gaze into those beautiful blue eyes, my chest tightens, and I know this is exactly where I want to be. "If you want me, sweetheart, you've got me. All of me."

"I feel the same. But, Micah—"

I smile. "I thought you believed in love at first sight."

"In fairy tales maybe," she says, "or in romance books, but in real life? Do you really think it's possible?"

"Can't we write our own romance story? A former Army-pilot-slash-auto-mechanic falls in love with a beautiful Irish-American runaway?"

She smiles. "That sounds wonderful."

"Then that's our story." I lean close to kiss her. "The rest we'll make up as we go along."

My phone rings then. "It's Chris," I tell Robyn as I take the call. "He's calling with an update. Chris, I'm going to put you on speaker so Robyn can hear, too."

"I'm here at the hospital now," he says. They're all going to be okay. Tony and Ricky are both in surgery and in stable condition. My deputy was treated and released, and she's resting at home."

"Thanks for the update, Chris," I say as we end the call.

"Can we go to the hospital tomorrow?" Robyn asks. "I'd like to see Tony, but I think I need to see Ricky, too. He tried to help me, and he almost died in the process. I need to thank him, at least, and say goodbye."

"Sure, we can go." I rise from the sofa, lifting her in my arms. "But right now, I think we should go to bed. It's late, and you've had a traumatic evening."

"So have you," she says, wrapping her arm around my neck.

After we get ready for bed, I turn off all the lights and set the alarm. Robyn slides under the covers, and I quickly join her. Immediately, she reaches for me. As I pull her close, I confirm my suspicions—she's naked.

"You're way overdressed," she says as she skims her hands over my hips.

"I wouldn't say *over*dressed." I've got boxer-briefs on and nothing else.

She rolls toward me and kisses me. It's a poignant kiss, tender and gentle, almost reverent. She cups my cheeks and brushes her thumbs over my lips.

"I've never been in love before," she says. "I've never

trusted anyone that much. But I trust you." She leans in to kiss me again, this time with more heat. "I want you," she whispers.

While I shove off my boxers, she reaches into the nightstand drawer and grabs a condom. I take it from her, rip the packet open, and quickly sheath myself. Before I can move, she's straddling me, hovering over my erection. She maintains eye contact as she slowly lowers herself on me. Her hair hangs loose, soft waves caressing my bare skin. This was my fantasy in the beginning—to feel her hair brushing my chest.

I groan as she sinks onto me, drawing me deeper into her tight heat. She's biting her lower lip in concentration. My hands go to her waist. I don't rush her or guide her. She knows what she's doing, and I'm happy to wait for her. But I need that physical contact. I need my hands on her.

I keep reminding myself we survived today. *She's okay. She's safe.*

If I allow myself to think about how close she came to injury tonight—or worse—I run the risk of losing my mind.

When she's worked herself on me, at least as far as she can go, she moans. And then she starts moving on me, lifting herself, settling down again, over and over as she finds her rhythm. Her pupils are dilated, her cheeks flushed pink. I reach up and run my fingers through her hair, watching the strands fall. I gather her hair in my hands and pull her closer for a kiss.

Our lips cling together, shaking and hungry. Our tongues tangle, our breaths mingle. Having her here with me, in my arms, in my bed, feels so right. This is what I've always craved—this kind of connection. As she moves faster and faster, angling herself just right, I feel the tension rise in her thighs. She's close to coming, and I pace myself, determined to hold off my own orgasm until she's found hers.

Her pussy tightens on me, squeezing me tightly, and she gasps as she presses her hot face into the crook of my neck. I slide my hands up and down her back as I murmur to her, telling her how beautiful she is, how much I want her. As she finally relaxes on me, I finally give myself permission to come. I surge up into her and give in to my need.

I roll us then so we're lying side by side. I brush back her hair and study her face, wanting to memorize every feature. We've shared our feelings tonight, but there's been no discussion of the future, and I don't want to make assumptions.

We must be on the same wavelength, because she says, "It looks like you're stuck with me now."

My breath catches in my chest. "Does this mean you've changed your mind about leaving Colorado?"

"With Verne out of the picture, there's no need for me to go. Not when I feel like I'm building something here… with you. I don't want to leave you. I've been here only a short time, but this feels like home. It's more of a home to me than I've ever had."

My heart slams into my ribs at the realization she's including me in her plans. There's an *us* now.

# 23

## Robyn

The next morning, Micah and I go to the hospital to see Tony and Ricky. We stop in Tony's room first, to see how he's doing.

"Hey, guys!" he says when we walk into his room. Tony's lying propped up, his head on a stack of pillows.

Cara is seated at his bedside.

Micah walks over to the bed and shakes Tony's hand. "I'm glad to see you awake and smiling."

"It's these awesome painkillers," Tony says. "They're

some good stuff. I'm feelin' no pain."

"Hi, Tony," I say as I join Micah at the bedside. "I'm so sorry—"

"Hey, none of that," he says with a dismissive wave. "It's not your fault."

I reach for his hand and give it a gentle squeeze. "I'm glad you're all right."

"I get a few days off work. What's bad about that?"

"You can take more than a few days," Micah says. "Take as much time as you need."

I notice Cara eyeing me sheepishly. Hoping we can have a fresh start, I offer her a smile. "Hi, Cara."

To my surprise, she smiles back. "Hi, Robyn. I'm glad you're safe. Tony told me what happened yesterday. It sounds awful. You must have been terrified."

"It was pretty intense." I nod to Tony. "I'm just glad he's okay."

While the guys chat for a bit, Cara and I exchange a few more words. It looks like the animosity between us is gone, and I'm glad. There's no reason we can't be friends.

When a nurse comes in to check Tony's vitals, Micah and I get ready to take our leave.

Micah wags his finger at Tony. "Don't come back to work until you're one hundred percent back to normal, all right?" He turns to Cara. "Make sure he listens, Cara."

We leave Tony's room and stop at a nurses' station to ask where we can find Ricky.

"He's being kept in a secured room down the hall, with a police guard," she says, giving us the room number. "I doubt they'll let you talk to him."

We head to his room anyway just in case they'll let me talk to him. Dennis, one of Chris's deputies, is standing guard outside the room.

"Can I talk to him?" I ask the deputy as I peer through the window. Ricky is lying in bed, and I notice one of his wrists and an ankle are handcuffed to the bedframe. He looks pale and there are dark circles under his eyes. At least his hair is freshly washed and combed.

He frowns. "I'm sorry, but he's under arrest. I'm not supposed to let anyone in there, other than medical staff and law enforcement."

"Come on, Dennis," Micah says. "She just wants to talk to him for five minutes. You can stand right there by the bed."

"Fine. But just five minutes. Not a second longer."

Dennis follows us into the room and stands at the foot of the bed.

Ricky's eyes widen when he spots me. "Robyn!"

"Hey, Ricky."

"You're okay?" he asks.

I nod. "I'm fine. How are you?"

He tries to shift his position and winces in the process. "Pretty sore. But the doctor says I'll live." He glances up at Micah, who's standing beside me, then back at me. "I'm glad you came. I wanted to tell you I'm sorry, Robyn, for everything. I never meant to put you in danger. Everything just sort of snowballed out of control."

"I know you didn't. Drugs have a way of clouding someone's judgement."

He nods. "I'm detoxing. It's been rough, but it's necessary." He pauses a moment. "It looks like I'm going to jail."

"I figured you were."

"Yeah. Besides dealing drugs, I'm being charged as an accomplice to attempted murder. But, Robyn, I swear I never would have hurt you, no matter how strung out I got. I still consider you my best friend." His eyes tear up. "Some friend I turned out to be, right?"

My throat tightens painfully. "You were a good friend when I needed you most. When you protected me from the older boys, and when you protected me from Doug. I'll always be grateful to you for that."

"Thanks." He winces in pain. "Are you doing okay now?" He glances again at Micah. "Are you safe here? Are you happy?"

"I am." I smile when Micah squeezes my shoulders. "Very happy. In fact, I'm staying."

"I'm glad. There's not much for you back in Denver. It makes me happy knowing you're happy."

"Sorry, but it's time to go," the deputy says. He nods to the door.

I stand next to Ricky's bed and reach down to squeeze his shackled hand. "I wish you well, Ricky. Take care." Now my eyes are tearing up. I imagine this is the last time I'll see him.

Wiping his eyes with his free hand, he nods. "You, too, Robyn." He gazes up at Micah. "Take good care of her."

"I will," Micah says as he takes my hand.

When we walk out of the room with the deputy, Chris is waiting for us in the hallway.

"She just wanted to say goodbye to him," Dennis tells the sheriff.

"It's fine," Chris says. To us, he says, "Can you both come to the station to give a deposition? Ricky has indicated he's going to plead guilty to any charges, and the DEA has enough evidence on Verne to arrest and charge him. But they're going to need depositions from both of you related to what happened last night."

Micah looks at me for confirmation, and I nod. "Yeah," he says. "We'll go now and get it over with."

"Thanks, guys."

I hold it together until we get out to the truck. That's when I finally break down. Micah holds me as I cry.

* * *

Micah finishes working on my car Wednesday morning. The first thing I do, after thanking him, is drive it to the nearest gas station to fill up the tank. It's such a relief to have my own transportation again—not that I have anywhere I need to go. But at least now I can drive myself to work and not inconvenience Micah. Although, to be honest, I kind of like him dropping me off and picking me up. Especially the picking me up part. That's been the highlight of my day, to see him walk in, looking so handsome and sexy in his black leather jacket, knowing he's there *for me*.

That afternoon, I drive myself to work.

I'm settling in quickly to my new job as a server at Ruth's Tavern. Jess, another server, takes me under her wing, answering questions and offering advice.

Someone plays an Adele song on the jukebox, and I remember when Micah and I danced here. That was the start of everything. Just that connection, holding each other for something as simple as a slow dance, opened a floodgate of emotions.

I go about my business, taking and delivering orders. Traffic picks up around five o'clock, the beginning of the dinner rush. I recognize some of the customers who come in, mostly having seen them before at the diner. A few of them wave to me or come up and say hi.

Killian and Hannah stop in for dinner. Ruth and Jack sit down at a booth with them for a little while to chat. As I walk by them, I hear snippets of what sounds like wedding plans. I guess someone's getting married soon. I'm guessing it's Hannah and Killian because Micah's never mentioned anything about his sister and Jack getting married.

At six, Tommy Hoffman returns to the tavern and claims a booth. Jess takes his order, and I do my best to avoid him entirely. Unfortunately, he's making it difficult. I feel his eyes on me for the next hour. After eating a steak and a baked potato, he nurses a couple of beers, followed by a shot of whiskey.

As I walk past his table, Tommy reaches out and snags my forearm. "Hey, sugar, when do you get a break?"

He really does think he's God's gift to women.

"Excuse me," I say as I try to pull away.

He stands to block my path. "Hey, don't rush off so fast."

"I'm working." I'd think that was obvious.

"Your talents are being wasted here, sugar." His gaze drops to my chest. "Come work for me, and I promise you I'll make it worth your while."

"No thanks," I say.

Suddenly, I feel a presence behind me as a comforting hand settles on my shoulder.

"Let her go, Hoffman," Micah says in a tight voice.

Tommy grins at Micah. "You going to make me, *half breed*?"

The insult has me seeing red. "Don't you dare call him—"

Micah grabs Tommy's wrist and squeezes hard. Wincing, he instantly releases my arm.

Micah gently steers me out of the way.

Then Tommy takes a swing at Micah and misses. He growls in outrage and tries again, only to fail a second time, which pisses him off more.

Micah grabs Tommy by his shirt collar, swings him around, and pushes his back against a pillar. "Touch her again and—"

"And what, *half breed*? What are you going to do about it?"

"Try me and see, asshole." Micah presses his forearm against Tommy's throat, cutting off his air. That shuts him up real quick.

A second later, Jack's there, pulling Micah back. "That's enough, guys. You know the rules. No fighting in Ruth's tavern." Jack glances back at me. "You okay, Robyn?"

"Yes."

Jack sets his gaze on Tommy. "You've worn out your welcome. Get out, and don't come back."

Tommy's glaring at both Jack and Micah.

Jack gets in his face. "Push me and see what happens."

"Assholes!" Tommy grabs his coat and storms out the door.

After Jack leaves us, Micah inspects my arm. "Did he hurt you?"

"It's sore, but I'm fine. Why are you here?"

"I'm hungry. And I miss you."

*Aww.* "Really?"

"Can you take a break and eat with me?" he asks.

Before I can say *no, I'm working,* Ruth is there beside me. "Yes, she can." She pats my back. "It's okay, Robyn. I saw what happened. Take a break and eat."

I wash up in the employees' lounge and remove my apron. I'm hungry, and getting to eat dinner with Micah is an unexpected bonus. I find him seated at a booth, and I slide in beside him. He smiles at me before leaning in for a kiss.

Jess comes to our table to take our orders. Micah asks for his usual—a burger and fries—and I go for the chicken tenders. We both order soft drinks.

It's not too long before Jess brings our food.

"So, who's getting married?" I ask. "I overheard Hannah and Killian talking wedding stuff with your sister and Jack."

"Hannah and Killian are tying the knot in a couple of weeks. It's a small wedding to be held at the lodge, just family and friends. Well, not that small," he says, chuckling. "Her entire family is coming out here from Chicago, and there are a lot of them. Killian's family is coming as well. Would you like to come with me as my plus one?"

I smile. "Really? You're inviting me to a wedding?"

"Of course. Will you be my date?"

"I'd love to, but I don't have a dress for something like

that."

"That's okay. We can go shopping for a dress in Estes Park."

Micah offers to pay for our meals, but Ruth says they're on the house.

"I guess I'll see you when you get home tonight," Micah says as he leans in and kisses me.

Someone at the bar whistles at us—most likely Jack—and I pull away, blushing.

"See you in a few hours," Micah says as he slips on his leather jacket. I watch him walk to the door, my eyes following him until he disappears from sight.

"You're smiling," Jess says with a grin as she walks past me.

Yes, I am. Micah has a way of making me do that.

# 24

## Robyn

*Three weeks later*

"Is this okay?" I ask Micah as I model the dress I'm wearing to Hannah and Killian's wedding. Maya took me dress shopping in Estes Park last weekend, and I ended up choosing a sage green maxi dress with long sleeves and a white collar. Maya said this shade of green compliments my hair color and my eyes. I paired the dress with low-heeled brown leather ankle boots. If I'm going to risk my neck by dancing, I don't want to do it in high heels.

Micah puts his hands on my hips and leans in to whisper, "You look beautiful, Robyn."

"No, you're the one who looks beautiful." I turn in his arms to admire him in his wedding attire—a black tuxedo with a white dress shirt and a turquoise tie and cummerbund. His hair is neatly braided, and he looks ridiculously handsome.

Micah's in the wedding party, along with Owen Ramsey, who is Killian's best man. Micah, John Burke, Jack, and one of Hannah's brothers—Shane—are the groomsmen.

"Does this mean I'll have to sit alone, since you'll be in the wedding party?"

"You won't be alone," he says. "You can sit with Jenny and Ruth."

His hands slide up to touch my hair, and I swat them away. "Don't you dare mess up my hair. It took me ages to get it like this." I put my hair up in a messy top knot and let some curling tendrils hang down. I had to watch a YouTube video three times just to figure out how to do it. I wanted to look nice today, sophisticated.

Micah checks the time. "Shall we?" he asks as he offers me his arm.

"Do I have a choice?"

He chuckles. "Don't be nervous. These are my friends, and they love you."

After we bundle up, we step out onto the cabin's porch. It snowed last night, and there's a good six inches of pristine white snow blanketing the ground. When Micah swoops me up in his arms, I squeal in surprise. He carries me to the truck, which is parked by the cabin.

"My hero," I say as he gently sets me on my seat.

He leans in to kiss me. "I didn't want you to get your new boots or your dress wet."

It's a 10-minute drive to the McIntyre Wilderness Lodge, where the wedding's being held. Hannah and Killian closed the lodge for the entire weekend so it's just their family and friends in attendance. I'm expecting a pretty small group until I see a whole row of shiny, black Cadillac Escalades parked in front of the lodge.

"Where did those come from?" I ask.

"Hannah's entire family flew in last night from Chicago. I imagine those are all their rentals."

I count five of the huge SUVs. "She must have a big family."

Micah chuckles. "You could say that. Besides her parents, her six siblings are here, plus their partners, and a whole bunch of kids."

Micah parks near the front entrance, and fortunately, the pavement has been shoveled clean, so I manage to keep my shoes dry as I walk in.

When we step through the double doors into the massive foyer, it's total chaos. Two little boys are chasing each other, and they're followed by two squealing, dark-haired little girls in flouncy pink dresses. The girls are obviously identical twins, maybe two years old. The boys are a little older.

One of the little girls loses her balance and falls to the floor. When she lets out a wail, the older of the two boys rushes to her side and picks her up.

"It's okay, Emmy," he says, hugging her close and patting her back.

The other twin, who looks on the verge of crying herself, clings to the boy's pantleg. The boy, who can't be more than eight, leans down and picks up the other girl, holding one on each of his hips.

"That's Aiden," Micah says. "And his twin sisters, Emerly and Everly. Jake McIntyre, Hannah's second oldest brother, is their father."

The other little boy, who looks to be about three or four, is blond with blue eyes.

"The blond is Luke," Micah says. "He's Shane McIntyre's son."

A gorgeous, petite blonde walks down the curved staircase, accompanied by a dark-haired guy. "What's all the caterwauling about?" she asks.

"That's Hannah's sister, Lia, and her husband—"

"Holy crap! Is that who I think it is?" I recognize the man holding hands with the blonde girl. I've seen him pop up on my social media feed a million times. It seems like every time I turn around, he has another hit song playing on the radio.

"Yeah, that's Jonah Locke. He's married to Lia McIntyre."

Another man—a huge, dark-haired guy with muscles that won't quit—jogs down the staircase, bypassing Lia and her husband, and heads right for the crying baby girl. "What happened?" he asks the boy as he takes the girl into his arms and looks her over. She clings to him like a little monkey, burying her face in the crook of his neck.

Aiden shrugs. "She fell down. I don't think she's hurt. I think it mostly scared her."

"That's Jake McIntyre," Micah says to me.

The man is huge, all muscles and well over six feet tall.

"Micah, please tell me there won't be a quiz. I'm already lost."

Micah chuckles. "This isn't all of them. The rest are probably upstairs." He takes my hand. "Let's go up. The wedding is taking place in the lounge."

We climb the staircase to the second floor and walk right into a spacious room that's been decorated for a wedding. There's a podium at one end, right in front of the massive stone hearth and woodburning fireplace. Facing the podium are rows of white folding chairs. The backs of the chairs have been adorned with boughs of ivy and cream and teal flowers. There are bouquets of fresh-cut cream-colored roses in crystal vases scattered throughout the room.

"It's beautiful," I say. Simple, yet lovely, like a fairytale. Classical music plays quietly over a speaker system set up by a DJ in the corner of the room. I glance out the wall of windows to our left at the enclosed courtyard, and it's a winter wonderland scene.

A striking man with short gray hair, dressed in a black tux and white dress shirt, walks up to us and shakes Micah's hand. "You'll find the groomsmen in the next room, giving Killian a hard time." Then he turns to me. "I'm Daniel Cooper. I'm officiating the ceremony. You must be the lovely Robyn I've been hearing about all morning."

I feel my cheeks heat. "I doubt that, but yes, I'm Robyn."

"There's a seat reserved for you, young lady. If you'll allow me, I'll take you to it."

"I'll see you after the ceremony," Micah says as he squeezes my hand. "Save the first dance for me, got it?"

I shoo him away. "Go do your wedding party stuff. I'll be fine."

When Micah leaves to join the other groomsmen, the silver fox offers me his arm. "Right this way."

He escorts me to the second row left of the center aisle, where Ruth and Jenny are already seated. I'm relieved to see some familiar faces.

"Here she is, ladies," he says to them. "As promised."

Jenny shoots to her feet and hugs me. "Robyn! You look stunning."

The compliment makes me smile. I haven't seen Jenny since the day I quit working at the diner. "You're still speaking to me," I say, a huge weight lifted off my chest.

"Of course I am," she says, laughing as she releases me and instead holds my hands. "Ruth told me what happened—that you found out Micah asked me to hire you, and you refused to go along with it. I understood completely, and I'm happy it worked out perfectly for you and Ruth. No hard feelings, okay?"

I nod, feeling massively relieved. "None at all. Thank you."

Ruth stands. "You look lovely, Robyn. That dress compliments your hair beautifully." She motions me forward. "Here, sit between us."

Once I'm seated, I have a chance to really look around the room. The silver fox—I think he said his name was Dan something, or Cooper—is standing at the front of the room. A good-looking younger red-haired guy walks up and puts his arm around Cooper, leans in and whispers something in the silver fox's ear. Cooper smiles at him, and I could swear the guy is blushing.

The seats fill up with guests, some of the ones I saw just a few minutes ago downstairs, plus a lot more people. There's a pretty blonde woman holding a brown-haired baby girl on her hip. Another couple have a baby girl, and obviously another one on the way because the woman is clearly pregnant. Yet another couple, both of them tall, the woman quite statuesque, and the man towers over everyone. He's holding a dark-haired baby girl in his arms.

Two older women are seated right in front of us, in

the front row.

After that, everything happens in a blur. Killian, dressed in a tuxedo, walks in, along with his groomsmen, Micah among them, looking strikingly handsome in his tuxedo.

Killian shakes hands with Cooper, who pats him on the back.

The music transitions then into a wedding march, and the room falls quiet.

The two boys we saw downstairs walk down the aisle. First the older boy, Aiden, I think his name is, followed by the little blond boy, who's tossing cream rose petals on the floor. The bridal party is next, all of them beautiful in pale teal dresses.

Hannah, looking amazing in a traditional white wedding gown, is being escorted down the aisle by another silver fox. I'm assuming he's her dad.

"That's Calum McIntyre," Ruth whispers to me. "Hannah's father. And this is Hannah's mother, Bridget." She points at one of the women seated in front of us, a petite lady with strawberry-blonde hair.

I wonder what it's like to grow up in such a large family. They appear to be really close, everyone chatting and laughing, chasing after kids. As an only child, I can't really relate. I look toward the front of the room, and Micah meets my gaze, a smile on his face. For a moment, I imagine what our child might look like. Warm brown skin with either dark hair, or maybe auburn like mine. With his dark eyes, or maybe blue.

I hear a baby crying somewhere behind me, followed by soft shushing noises.

Hannah has reached the front of the room now, and her father hugs her and kisses her cheek before he lays her hand in Killian's.

I've never been to a wedding before, so this is a lot to take in. I don't even know most of these people.

The vows are short and succinct. No promises of anyone obeying anyone, just promises to love, honor, and cherish in sickness and in health. When Cooper tells the happy couple they can kiss, they do—wow, do they kiss. And the guests start clapping. It's a joyful ceremony, and Hannah and Killian look incredibly happy.

Cooper addresses the audience. "And now, if you'll all make your way downstairs to the restaurant let's see if we can put a dent in all that food."

\* \* \*

When the crowd breaks up, Micah makes his way to me, a huge smile on his face. "You survived," he says with a chuckle.

"Yes, thanks to your sister and Jenny. By the way, she's not holding a grudge against me for quitting on her."

"Of course she isn't," he says, as he links our arms as we head downstairs to the restaurant.

We mingle in the dining room and snack on hot finger foods. Micah takes me around and introduces me to all the people I haven't met—and there are a lot of them. Everyone's super friendly. The kids are adorable, and they're the center of attention.

After we have cake, Hannah tosses her wedding bouquet into a crowd of women. Not me—I stay far away from that, despite all the people who encourage me to join in. When Jenny catches the flowers, everyone cheers, and Jenny blushes.

When we return to the lounge upstairs, the chairs have been cleared away, and the DJ is playing music. There's a bar set up in another corner of the room, and Ruth and Jack are passing out drinks.

"This is my dance," Micah says as he pulls me into his arms and we start to sway to the music. He leans in and kisses my temple, then whispers, "They're all my dances."

But then Chris cuts in and steals a dance, and Micah just shakes his head before he goes to dance with Jenny.

"You look very handsome today," I tell him. He's wearing a charcoal gray suit with a white dress shirt and a black tie. "I'm so used to seeing you in your uniform."

Chris smiles. "You look lovely, and Micah can't keep his eyes off you."

Then Killian asks me to dance, and I notice Micah dancing with the bride. Finally, Micah and I find our way back together, in each other's arms.

"No more cutting in," he tells me. "The next guy who wants to dance with you will have to fight me over it."

The DJ plays some snappy Cajun music, and Killian dances with an attractive older woman.

"That's his mom," Micah tells me. "She and his grandparents came all the way from Louisiana for the wedding."

"Who are they?" I ask, pointing to a couple who are dancing with their children in their arms. The man, who's dressed in a tux as he was one of the groomsmen, is holding the little blond-haired boy I saw running around earlier. The woman, a pretty blonde with the most amazing blue-green eyes, is holding a baby girl.

"That's Shane McIntyre and his wife, Beth, along with

their kids, Luke and Ava. Shane provided the funding for Hannah and Killian to purchase this lodge and start their business."

"Oh. He's the one who bought the helicopter."

"Right. He's the head honcho of a security company based in Chicago."

I glance across the room to see Ruth dancing with Jack. "Do you think they'll get married?" I nod toward his sister.

Micah shrugs. "They will if Ruth decides she wants to." He takes my hand and spins me. "What about you?" he asks as he pulls me back into his arms. "Do you see yourself getting married one day?"

I gaze up at him, at those mesmerizing, dark eyes. He's the most handsome man I've ever known. "I used to think not. Other than my parents, I never saw a married couple that really loved each other. But now—" I break off, afraid to say the words out loud.

He slides his fingers into my hair. "But now?"

"I'm starting to see the appeal."

He smiles just before he kisses me on the dance floor in front of his sister and all his friends.

* * *

Sunday evening, I surprise Micah with a road trip to Estes Park. "I hope you like barbeque," I say.

He chuckles. "Does a bear—well, you know—in the woods?"

"Good." I drive us to a popular restaurant in town. I asked Maya for recommendations, and this is the one she came up with.

"He'll love it," she said. "But make sure you get reservations, or you'll be waiting for ages to get seated."

So here we are. Thanks to our reservations, we're seated right away at a cozy table for two in the corner. It's a nice, upscale restaurant with candles on the table. We both order the beef brisket, some sides to share, and beer from a popular local brewery.

While we're sitting here waiting for our food to arrive, I'm fighting a huge grin. Over the past few weeks, I've made several smaller payments to Micah in my effort to reimburse him for the transmission and the new tires, but tonight's the final payment. This is the biggest expense I've ever had in my life, and I feel so darn good knowing this is my last payment to him. I did it!

"What's the special occasion?" he asks, starting to look a bit concerned. "I didn't forget something, did I?"

"No, relax." I pull out my phone and tap a few times. A

moment later, his phone chimes with a notification. "Go ahead. Check it."

He glances at his phone screen, smiles, and then looks back at me. "Thank you, Robyn." He reaches for my hand. "You didn't have to, but I know it's important to you, so congratulations."

"You're welcome." I sent him $800 via Apple Cash. "That's my last payment. That covers everything—the transmission, including labor, and the new tires."

He's told me repeatedly that I didn't have to pay him back, but of course I do. This is important to me.

Our food arrives then, and we eat. The beef brisket is tender and amazing. Everything is delicious, including dessert, a giant slice of chocolate cake I manage to talk him into sharing with me. The setting is beautiful. I've paid him back. Everything's perfect.

Including the way he's looking at me.

Our server stops by to refill our water glasses. "So, is this a special occasion?"

"It is," Micah says as he winks at me.

"Congratulations, then," the guy says. "You make a beautiful couple."

Micah's eyes are locked on mine. "Thanks. I think so, too."

I feel my cheeks heating up, but I can't bring myself to look away.

After the server leaves, Micah reaches into his pocket and withdraws a small emerald-green velvet box. He holds out his hand, and when I give him mine, he sets the box on my palm. "I was planning a bit of a surprise tonight myself."

My heart is pounding as I gaze down at the little box.

"Go ahead and open it," he says.

My fingers are shaking as I pry the lid up. Nestled inside is a slim gold band set with a gorgeous, clear blue gemstone.

"It's aquamarine," he says. "The same color as your eyes."

I stare at the ring. "Micah, it's gorgeous."

"It's a token of my feelings—a promise ring. I realize it's too soon for anything official, but I wanted to give you something. Will you wear it?"

"Yes."

He removes the ring from the box, and as I hold out my left hand, he slips the ring on my finger. It fits perfectly. "How did you know my size?"

He grins. "Lucky guess."

# Epilogue

### Robyn

*In the spring*

"I really wish you'd reconsider," Micah says for the third time today. It's Sunday, and we're both off work. And I have big plans today with Maya. And with Travis and Killian and Hannah.

We're seated at the kitchen table finishing up a late breakfast, which I made myself—French toast and bacon.

"It'll be fun, Micah. Don't be such a party pooper."

"Party pooper?" His eyebrows rise sharply, as if I said something utterly ridiculous. "You think me being a bit worried because you're climbing a 30-foot tall rock makes me a party pooper?" He leans back in his chair and crosses his arms over his chest—aggressively. "How about it makes me a concerned boyfriend? One who doesn't want his girlfriend getting *hurt?*"

"Please don't be like this. I like Maya. I like that we're becoming friends. And I *want* to learn how to climb. Besides, she's an expert. And so are Travis and Killian and Hannah. They'll all be there, too. It'll be fine."

"Do you realize how high thirty feet is? If you fall—"

"Killian is going to belay me. *If* I fall, he'll handle it. But maybe I won't fall. Maybe I'll be good at this. Have you thought of that?"

Micah scrubs his hands over his face and exhales heavily. "Are you *trying* to give me a heart attack?"

"No." It's hard not to snicker in the face of such melodrama. Micah's not afraid of anything, but when it comes to me, he's definitely overprotective. I pull his hands off his face, cupping them in mine, and make him look at me. "I really want to do this. I'm not afraid, so please don't be afraid for me. Have a little faith. You know Killian won't let me get hurt, and Maya is a great instructor."

He gives me his *I-am-being-reasonable* face. "But this is thirty feet we're talking about, Robyn. That's equivalent to a three-story building. Pardon me if I'm a bit freaked out."

Maya has taken me out climbing a few times already, but the highest I've gone is fifteen feet. This climb is definitely higher. Definitely next-level stuff. "Just be glad we're not free soloing it."

"No," he says sharply, straightening in his chair. "Absolutely not. Don't even joke about it."

I stand and move closer, stepping between his legs so I can cup his face and lean in. "Just kidding." And then I kiss him. "Now, let's get ready to go. We're supposed to meet them at the rock face in thirty minutes."

"Fine," he mutters. "Get your gear."

We grab our jackets. It's a nice spring day, and the sun is out, so it's warm enough to climb comfortably in a long-sleeve T-shirt and leggings. I reach for my backpack, which is already packed with my climbing gear and shoes, and follow Micah out to the truck. It's a 15-minute drive to the trailhead, then an easy 10-minute hike to the climb site—a vertical rock face popular with locals and tourists.

Micah's quiet on the drive over, and I feel bad that he's genuinely worried about my safety. I lay my hand on his thigh, hoping to reassure him, and without saying a word, he lays his on mine.

We park at the trail head and set off to our destination. A couple of minutes into our walk, we hear someone coming up behind us.

"Wait up, guys!" Hannah says.

I glance back to see Hannah and Killian gaining on us. "Hello, Mrs. Deveraux," I say as she comes alongside me. It's hard to believe they've been married for six months already.

Hannah smiles as she squeezes my shoulder. "Are you ready for this?"

"I am. I can't say the same for Micah, but I'm good to go."

Killian walks up to Micah and claps him on the back. "It'll be fine, Micah. I promise not to let your girlfriend fall."

Micah tightens his grip on my hand. "Who's worried?" he asks, totally bluffing. "I'm not."

When we arrive at the rock face, Maya and Travis are already there setting up. Since this is a popular site for climbing, there are already anchors set in the rock face. Maya's up there right now setting the top ropes for the both of us. I crane my neck up to see her and realize just how high thirty feet is. *Wow. That's high.* My stomach takes a dive, and I feel a bit dizzy.

"Hey, perfect timing!" Maya calls from above. "I'm coming down now, Trav."

"Coming down," he repeats, letting her know he's ready. He braces himself as she begins to descend, letting out rope as she rappels down.

Micah helps me put on my harness and attach my carabiners and other equipment. Killian supervises as I thread my rope through the belay device and lock the loop in the carabiner. He does the same for himself, and then we do a safety check. Maya is a stickler for safety protocols, and she's drilled them into my head.

Travis and Maya do the same. After we double-check our knots and harnesses, we're good to go.

I remove my hiking boots and strap on my climbing shoes—slim, flexible sport shoes designed to allow my toes to find and grip even small crevices. Mine are black and teal.

"Are you ready?" Maya asks. "It's like we've done before, just a little bit higher. Piece of cake, right?"

I crane my neck to see the top of the face we're about to climb. It does look awfully high.

Micah walks up behind me and lays his hands on my shoulders. "You don't have to do this if you don't want to," he whispers in my ear.

I tilt my head back to see his face. "I'm good."

Micah kisses me, and then he steps back to let Killian pick up the belaying line. Travis has Maya's line. I know she could easily climb this rock without any support, but since she's teaching me, she lets Travis belay her.

"Ready?" Travis asks Maya.

She gives him a thumbs up.

"Ready, Robyn?" Killian asks me.

I nod. "Yep. I'm ready." I'm excited, but I'm also nervous. I glance back at Micah, who has moved back a bit to give Killian and Travis room to move. When I catch his gaze, Micah nods to me.

Maya starts off by raising her foot and placing it in a crevice at about knee height. I copy her and do the same, although it takes me longer to find a suitable starting place.

As I step up, I feel Killian taking up the slack in the line. It's reassuring to know he's holding my line. If I slip, he'll stop my fall, and I'll either find new footing or he'll lower me safely to the ground.

Maya keeps pace with me, moving at my speed, watching my moves and offering advice.

"You're doing great, Robyn!" Hannah calls from the ground.

I glance down to see Micah and Hannah standing together, back a few yards from Killian and Travis, giving them plenty of room to maneuver. I'm overwhelmed with gratitude for these new people in my life. Not just Micah, but the others as well. His friends have all embraced me into their lives, into their world. They've made me feel welcome, and now they're teaching me new skills. Hannah's already asked me if I want to join the McIntyre Search and Rescue team.

I'm about halfway up the rock face when my foot slips. As I abruptly drop a few feet, my heart shoots up in my throat. But the line quickly goes taut, stopping my descent. I brace my feet against the rock to steady myself.

"You okay?" Maya asks me. She's about six feet above me now, looking down.

"Yeah, I'm fine. Just give me a minute." I take a couple of deep breaths to slow my breathing. I don't dare glance down at the ground, or I'll lose my nerve.

"It's okay, Robyn," Killian says from the ground as he adjusts his stance. His steady voice is reassuring. "You're doing great."

"Come on, O'Neil, pick up the pace," Maya says as she starts ascending once more. "We don't have all day." She's a tough love kind of girl, and that's exactly what I need right now.

I find new hand and foot holds and start ascending once more. It's a steady climb up, no more slipping, until I reach the top. Maya's waiting for me there. She extends her arm toward me, offering me a high-five. I smack my palm against hers.

"You did it!" Maya says. "You should be proud of yourself. I know Micah's proud of you." She glances down at the ground. "You're proud of her, aren't you, Micah?" she yells down.

"You better believe I am!" he yells back.

We start our descent then, and of course it goes a little quicker on the way down than it did going up. When I'm a couple of feet above the ground, I feel a pair of hands grasp me around the waist. I look back to see Micah smiling at me.

"You were awesome," he says as he lowers me to the ground. "You took two years off my life when you fell, but other than that—you kicked ass."

I turn to face him, and he wraps his arms around me. "I like climbing."

He winces. "I was afraid you were going to say that."

Maya slaps Micah on the back. "She did great."

After we pack up all our gear, I change back into my

hiking boots. The six of us hike back to the parking lot.

"Lunch is on me," Maya says. She winks at me. "Let's go celebrate Robyn's accomplishment."

* * *

"Were you scared?" Micah asks me that night as we're lying in bed.

"Yeah, a little. But I knew I was in good hands. I knew Killian wouldn't let me fall."

"I assume you want to keep climbing?"

I nod. "Yes, sorry."

"Then I guess it's time I learn how to belay," he says. "I want to be the one holding your rope."

"Aww." I roll to face him and lay my arm across his chest. "That's so romantic."

He grins. "I'm just being practical. I think I'd be less nervous if I was belaying you myself. I hated just standing there and watching. I want to be more hands-on."

"Speaking of hands-on." I roll him to his back and straddle him. As I lean down to kiss him, my hair falls forward, brushing his bare skin. He shivers visibly. "I know you'll be there to catch me if I fall," I say.

"Always," he says, his tone solemn.

That sounds like a promise.

* * *

The next morning, while we're sitting at the kitchen table eating breakfast, Micah sets his laptop on the table in front of me. Zillow's on the screen.

"You know, the cabin is pretty small for two people," he says. "I was wondering if you'd be interested in looking at something larger? Maybe something with a few bedrooms and a couple of bathrooms? A larger kitchen and dining area maybe? What do you say? There are some new listings on here that look pretty good."

My eyes widen. "Are you talking about going house hunting?"

"Yeah." He shrugs like it's no big deal.

"Together?" I ask, clarifying. This is a huge step.

He winces. "Is it too soon?"

"I like the idea. It's just—"

He nods. "It's too soon."

"No! It's not. I—"

He comes around to my side of the table, pulls me to my feet, and then he takes my chair and sits me on his lap. He pushes my empty plate aside so he can bring the laptop closer. "Take a look at these and see if there are any that look good to you."

I turn to face him. "Are you serious?"

"Yes," he says. "Absolutely."

I smile. "You want to play house with me?"

He grins. "I do."

Those two little words make my heart stutter. "Those are pretty big words, mister."

Now it's his turn to smile. "I know. Do they scare you?"

I shake my head. "Not one bit."

"Good." He kisses the back of my hand. "Robyn O'Neil, will you pick out a house with me? Do you want to live with me forever and ever, 'til death do us part?"

I kiss him then, and murmur the words, "I do," against his smiling lips.

\* \* \*

Thank you for reading Robyn and Micah's story. I hope you are enjoying the *McIntyre Search and Rescue* series. More books are coming!

\* \* \*

If you'd like to receive free bonus content each month—exclusive for my newsletter subscribers—sign up for my newsletter on my website. You can also find links to my free short stories, information on upcoming releases, a reading order, and more. www.aprilwilsonauthor.com

\* \* \*

Here are links to my list of audiobooks: www.aprilwilsonauthor.com/audiobooks

\* \* \*

I interact daily with readers in my Facebook reader group (April Wilson Reader Group) where I post frequent updates and share teasers. Come join me!

\* \* \*

Books by April Wilson

**McIntyre Security Bodyguard Series**
*Vulnerable*
*Fearless*
*Shane–a novella*
*Broken*
*Shattered*
*Imperfect*
*Ruined*
*Hostage*

*Redeemed*
*Marry Me–a novella*
*Snowbound–a novella*
*Regret*
*With This Ring–a novella*
*Collateral Damage*
*Special Delivery*
*Vanished*
*Baby Makes 3*
*Wrecked*

## McIntyre Security Bodyguard Series Box Sets

*Box Set 1*
*Box Set 2*
*Box Set 3*
*Box Set 4*

## McIntyre Security Protectors

*Finding Layla*
*Damaged Goods*
*Freeing Ruby*

## McIntyre Search and Rescue

*Search and Rescue*
*Lost and Found*
*Tattered and Torn*

*Dark and Dangerous*
*Locked and Loaded*

**Tyler Jamison Novels**
*Somebody to Love*
*Somebody to Hold*
*Somebody to Cherish*

**Daddy Detectives (Tyler and Ian) Series**
*Daddy Detectives Episode 1*
*Daddy Detectives Episode 2*

**A British Billionaire Romance Series**
*Charmed*
*Captivated*

**Miscellaneous Books**
*Falling for His Bodyguard*

\* \* \*

Audiobooks by April Wilson
For links to my audiobooks, please visit my website:
www.aprilwilsonauthor.com/audiobooks

www.ingramcontent.com/pod-product-compliance
Ingram Content Group UK Ltd.
Pitfield, Milton Keynes, MK11 3LW, UK
UKHW041106020925
7684UKWH00008B/30